She was an absolute knockout.

"Good evening." She said it as sweetly as Red Riding Hood, but the twitch in her smile was nothing short of predatory. Before he could warn himself to be practical again, before he could rein in his hope that she'd come here for a reason that was as far away from professional as imaginable, his father's words revisited him like the Ghost of Longing Past.

You're also careful in the wrong ways. Being reckless is okay from time to time.

Opening the door wider, Royce decided to agree with his father's assessment. The world hadn't flown off the axis when he'd risked kissing Taylor—in fact, things had begun going his way.

He grinned, deciding that in this situation, he was a safe Big Bad Wolf to her Red Riding Hood. "Won't you come in?"

* * *

His Forbidden Kiss by Jessica Lemmon is the first book in the Kiss and Tell series.

Dear Reader,

Welcome to my new series, Kiss and Tell, where we will follow the Knox siblings (there are three: two brothers and a sister) through their journeys of finding love in the midst of running one of the biggest tech companies in the world.

Book ideas come to me in a variety of ways. Sometimes it's a line of spoken dialogue from one of the characters, other times it's a trope that captures my attention (forced proximity, anyone?) or, in the case of *His Forbidden Kiss*, a scene that jump-starts the story.

When I "met" Taylor Thompson, she was running away from a marriage proposal. In high heels and an elegant ball gown, no less! The image was so strong that I crafted an entire book around it. Why was she running? Who was she running from? Who saves her? That last part was easy: the hero who is *not* her date for the evening!

I had *so* much fun building the wealthy world of the Knoxes and crafting the fun yet tricky family dynamics between siblings. I hope you love reading these characters as much as I enjoyed creating them for you. If you'd like to learn more about my journey from billionaires and bad boys (and beyond!), come see me at www.jessicalemmon.com.

Happy reading!

Jessica

JESSICA LEMMON

HIS FORBIDDEN KISS

HARLEQUIN

DESIRE

PLEASE RECYCLE
THIS PRODUCT IS RECYCLABLE

Recycling programs
for this product may
not exist in your area.

ISBN-13: 978-1-335-20893-4

His Forbidden Kiss

Copyright © 2020 by Jessica Lemmon

This edition published by arrangement with Harlequin Books S.A.

For questions and comments about the quality of this book,
please contact us at CustomerService@Harlequin.com.

Harlequin Enterprises ULC
22 Adelaide St. West, 40th Floor
Toronto, Ontario M5H 4E3, Canada
www.Harlequin.com

Printed in U.S.A.

A former job-hopper, **Jessica Lemmon** resides in Ohio with her husband and rescue dog. She holds a degree in graphic design currently gathering dust in an impressive frame. When she's not writing supersexy heroes, she can be found cooking, drawing, drinking coffee (okay, wine) and eating potato chips. She firmly believes God gifts us with talents for a purpose, and with His help, you can create the life you want.

Jessica is a social media junkie who loves to hear from readers. You can learn more at jessicalemmon.com.

Books by Jessica Lemmon

Harlequin Desire

Dallas Billionaires Club

Lone Star Lovers
A Snowbound Scandal
A Christmas Proposition

The Bachelor Pact

Best Friends, Secret Lovers
Temporary to Tempted
One Night, White Lies
Christmas Seduction

Kiss and Tell

His Forbidden Kiss

Visit her Author Profile page at Harlequin.com, or jessicalemmon.com, for more titles.

You can also find Jessica Lemmon on Facebook, along with other Harlequin Desire authors, at Facebook.com/harlequindesireauthors!

For Denita. You are so, so missed.

One

Heartbeat pounding in her ears, heels of her designer shoes clacking on the marble flooring, Taylor Thompson ran as fast as she dared in the heavy, beaded, floor-length Versace gown. She'd chosen it specifically for the River Grove Valentine's Day gala, extravagant even for the high-end affair, but until the tapered skirt was strangling her ankles with each quickening step she hadn't imagined it'd be inhibiting her escape.

She tugged the hemline as high as her calves, steered clear of the ladies' room—no doubt teeming with primped, classy women who were also attending the gala—and ducked into the coatroom.

At least she'd thought it was a coat "room."

Now that she'd shut the door behind her, the tight, dark space felt more like a coat *cracker box.*

No matter. She just needed thirty seconds to herself, away from onlookers. Without having to pretend she didn't know she was about to be proposed to.

God. A proposal.

She'd attended the gala every year save one—the year she traveled to Miami during a college vacation with her friends—so she never thought much of going. She'd never thought of *not* going. It was what the kids of River Grove did.

Here, being wealthy wasn't an option, it was a requirement.

Her family had helped build this town—along with her date's, Brannon Knox's, family. The Thompsons and Knoxes were known for founding one of the biggest tech companies in the nation. The ThomKnox Group was started by her late father, Charles, and Brannon's father, Jack, some twenty-six years ago, when Taylor was two years old.

It seemed that tonight Brannon was attempting a merger of a different style.

"Brannon Knox, what were you thinking?"

To be fair, she should ask herself exactly the same question. When he'd asked her to come as his date tonight, she should have said no. Instead, she'd chickened out, agreeing to *one last* event before having the discussion she should have had with him three weeks ago. The one where she said something to the effect of, "This isn't working. Let's be friends."

Aware she couldn't finish out the party in the closet, Taylor considered her options. She couldn't dart into the ladies' room and face Mrs. Mueller or

Patsy Sheffield. They were sweet, and had been nothing but lovely after her father died last fall, but they were also…involved. She didn't need the entire town gossiping about her hiding from her date—and Patsy and Mrs. Mueller would happily start that rumor.

Was it considered a rumor if it was true?

If it hadn't been for her father losing his battle with cancer not so long ago, she probably never would've dated Brannon. They'd known each other a lifetime, but the attraction simply hadn't been there.

Explaining that to him was never going to be fun. *Sorry, Bran. I only dated you because I was sad and in some way hoped it'd please my father from beyond the grave.* Now with an engagement on the line, explaining to Bran that she should've said no—before tonight—would be more agonizing.

"Dammit!" Fists balled, she stomped one high heel into the floor in frustration. It was hot in here and the room was closing in on her.

Deciding to find a bigger space in which to gather her thoughts, she reached for the doorknob. Wiggling it once, then twice, didn't help. The third time wasn't the charm—the antique knob had an antique lock fixture that had engaged.

"Crap." Sweat beaded on her brow as she jiggled harder, and she suddenly wished she'd carried her clutch in with her instead of leaving it on the table in Addison's care. At least then she would've had the light from her phone.

She wasn't particularly claustrophobic, but the options of suffocating in a coat closet or passing out from panic weren't good ones.

The instant she'd observed Brannon admiring the ring nestled in the Tiffany & Co. blue box backstage, she should have handled the situation. Where was a time machine when she needed one?

She strained to hear music or voices. Not a single sound infiltrated her insulated new home. Giving up on the doorknob, she backed up to throw her shoulder into the panel and bust herself out, when the door swung open, easy as you please.

Silhouetted in the frame was a pair of imposing shoulders in a black tuxedo jacket, long legs in matching trousers, and above that shadowed, sharp jaw she could easily imagine a frown.

Brannon's older brother.

"Taylor? What the hell are you doing in here?" Curiosity lined Royce Knox's voice. Even though he wasn't yelling at her, and even though he scared her about as much as a passing butterfly, her building anxiety pushed forth a gusty breath.

"Royce, thank God." She gripped his forearms. Over the material of his jacket she could make out the corded muscle, the sinew that made up those damned attractive arms. Once, years ago, she'd stumbled on her way to the limo and he'd been there to catch her. She was sixteen years old when she gripped his arms then. They weren't as muscular or thick as they were now, but the fluttery feeling in her belly was the same. When it came to Royce, there was never any question if she was attracted to him. She totally was.

She hadn't missed her father's scolding glower at that party afterward. He'd told her under no uncertain terms to stay away from the older Knox brother. "He's too old for you."

Her father hadn't wanted the older, more serious Knox brother for Taylor. He'd dreamed of a union between her and the younger, more eager one. Brannon.

She yanked her hands from Royce's forearms, unsure if she was more troubled by inadvertently obeying her father's wishes and dating Brannon, or feeling an attraction for Royce she still couldn't deny. It was there, though—pounding in her bloodstream.

"I thought I was going to die in here," she mumbled into the tight, dark space.

A short grunt came from Royce's throat. "Highly unlikely. Bran's looking for you."

"I know." She pictured the engagement ring and her stomach did another somersault. "This was our last date."

"What?" Royce's alarmed question was interrupted by another voice. Bran's coming from down the corridor.

"Has anyone seen Taylor?"

Since the closet she'd sprinted into was around a corner, Bran hadn't seen her or his brother yet. Nor would he. She wasn't ready.

Taylor yanked Royce into the small space and pulled the door shut behind him, lock be damned. Suffocating in here might be better than facing the man who was about to go down on bended knee.

"Hey!" Royce protested as the door clicked. She

clapped her hand over his mouth, feeling the barest hint of stubble pushing past a sharp, clean shave—his preference. He reached for her wrist but froze when she gently shushed him. Together, they listened. Her to her erratic pulse sloshing in her ears and just under that, Brannon's receding voice as he continued his search.

She let out the breath she'd held and became aware of two things. Royce's long, blunt fingers covering the pulse point at her wrist and the feel of his warm exhalations on her hand that still covered his mouth.

"This is where my parents were engaged." Taylor's voice was soft with reminiscence. Royce couldn't make out her expression in the dim light but he could hear the sadness. "At the Valentine's Day gala. Mom said it was the most romantic night of her life."

His heart ached for Taylor and her mother. Losing Charles had been hard on all of them. The Knoxes and Thompsons had practically been family since Royce was in grade school.

"That's probably why he did it," she tacked on glumly. Before Royce could wonder if she'd found out about the surprise, she confirmed with, "Brannon."

Gently, he pulled her hand away from his mouth, the soft scent of her perfume tickling his nose. She smelled good—she always had whenever he'd been this close to her, which was a rare occasion. Charles had seen to that.

"You know," he said. "About the proposal."

"Not until very recently, but yes."

And she didn't sound the least bit happy about it. He couldn't dredge up surprise at hearing that. She'd been dating his younger brother for what? On and off for three weeks? When Brannon came to show him the ring, Royce's reaction had been immediate and it hadn't been favorable. Brannon led with his heart and Royce was more of a numbers guy, so he'd stuck to what he knew and told his brother the truth. *Seems soon in the time line for that, Bran.*

"It's too soon," Taylor echoed now and Royce could swear the feeling in his chest was akin to relief. Bran's plan to propose was a mistake. Anyone should date longer than three weeks before stepping into engagement territory.

"It was supposed to be a surprise. Who blew it?"

"I saw Bran admiring the ring."

"She's a beauty," Royce said of the diamond solitaire that was God only knew how many carats.

"He showed you?" She sounded almost anguished.

He released her wrist and felt for a light switch, which he found after a few failed attempts and moving Taylor one step left and then right. Once the light clicked on he could see three things: empty hangers, plastic bins containing, according to the labels, holiday Decorations, and Taylor's expression: simultaneously distraught and beautiful. The beauty he was used to; distraught was a new look for her.

Shoulder-length dark blond hair swept up for the event, her lips painted a shade of pink darker than her usual. Taylor fit into the world of class and wealth as well as any of them. They were accustomed to attending events like this one—to being trussed and preening for the elders in their midst. Royce had grown used to the game over the decades. He'd been groomed on how to behave—in life, at work. It came as second nature to him now. He supposed Taylor could say the same.

Even her sparkling gown couldn't hide the ribbon of seriousness strung through her, the ambition she couldn't mask with glitz and glam. That, in part, was why Bran's suggestion to marry her had taken Royce by such surprise. They'd seemed an odd fit from the start. Taylor was like an unofficial sister, a little older than their actual sister, Gia.

But then, he hadn't had a chance to think of Taylor any differently before her father declared her off-limits.

When Bran was insistent about continuing with the proposal, Royce accepted that he might not know Bran or Taylor as well as he'd thought. That maybe they were in love after all.

Until right now. Taylor didn't seem like a woman in love. Not with her breathing approaching fast to erratic and that note of worry in her voice. Royce wasn't the only one who believed an engagement was a bad idea.

"It's hot in here. Try the knob." She didn't wait for him, shoving him aside and twisting the knob back and forth. When that didn't work, she slapped the door, letting out a growl when it didn't magically swing open.

He put a hand on her shoulder, hoping to quell her

anxiety, which was due to more than being trapped in a closet. "It's a country club teeming with people, Taylor. Someone will come around in a few minutes. Take a deep breath."

"I can't. I'm wearing Spanx."

Whatever those were. She thrust her bottom lip out and he fought a smile. She'd be fine as soon as she started breathing.

"Do your best. We've got this. Watch me." He bent to meet her eyes but didn't have to bend much. She was a good eight inches shorter than his six foot four, but today her high-heeled shoes added some height— her lips almost came to his chin.

Her hazel eyes met his, and in the dim light of the closet he could see that she wasn't calm yet.

"Breathe with me," he told her in his gentlest voice.

She let out a shaky breath and took in another, making a soft O shape with her mouth as she blew it out. She did it once more but on her exhale a tear streaked down her cheek.

"I don't want to hurt his feelings, Royce." She gripped his tux's lapels.

"I know." He didn't know, but felt it best to agree.

"It's Dad's fault I said yes to a first date." She tugged harder on his jacket. "I never should've let things go this far. Bran is nice and well suited but..." She shook her head. "I was going to end things this weekend. I only agreed to come tonight to be polite."

"You don't have to explain."

A frown bisected her eyebrows when she repeated, "I don't want to hurt him."

"Taylor." When her eyes tracked to his he saw guilt reflected back at him. "You don't have to say yes to a marriage proposal to be polite." He hooked a thumb under her chin and tilted her face toward his, needing her to understand. "No matter what your father wanted."

She nodded, a small one, her hands still clutching his tuxedo coat. He should've stepped away but instead he lingered, content to have her full attention. Something he couldn't remember having before now.

"It's going to be okay. You'll see." He'd been on the brink of offering a few more generic platitudes, but whatever else was poised on the tip of his tongue never made it out of his mouth.

Not when Taylor put her lips on his and kissed him for all she was worth.

Hell, maybe for all *he* was worth.

Two

Royce told himself to stop kissing her. Told himself that she wasn't for him. She was the Thompson princess, and he the older heir to the Knox kingdom. No matter how poorly suited she and Bran were, or what she'd admitted to Royce in the privacy of the locked closet. He recited those reminders again and again but couldn't seem to leave the sanctity of her seeking mouth.

Her lips were too lush, too ripe. She tasted like champagne and sex. Really great sex. It'd been a while since he'd had really great sex, so he allowed himself a moment to explore. To remember... Maybe *discover* was a better word because he didn't find a single familiar memory to cling to in Taylor's kiss. He only found newness. Excitement. A certain zest... If that was the right phrase.

Ah, screw it.

Who cared what it was called. Now that he'd tasted her, he was inclined to taste her a little longer. To indulge in what he'd been forbidden to claim. Though technically it was Taylor who'd claimed him. He was practically an innocent bystander.

Until he cupped the back of her neck. Until he swept his tongue into her mouth and sampled her deeply—giving in to the yearning that was only seconds old, but felt as if it'd been there a hell of a lot longer.

Royce valued control in all facets of his well-organized life. He'd always assumed it was the way he was wired—he'd inherited his father's shrewd business intelligence, where Brannon mirrored his father's excitement and spontaneity. The attributes had been divvied between the Knox sons equally and were doled out double to Gia—which was unfair, but nonetheless true.

Budgets and financial strategies made sense to him. Royce liked his role as CFO because it was predictable—math didn't have "gray areas."

Taylor *was* a gray area.

At ThomKnox, he'd carved out his dream career by age twenty-three. He was hailed a boy genius in this magazine or that blog post but he didn't care for monikers or attention. He kept his focus on the numbers, which never lied. Gossip websites couldn't claim the same.

Wouldn't they have a heyday if they found out you were making out with your younger brother's date?

That quiet reminder stopped him short of pushing Taylor against the nearest flat surface—the door in this case—and trailing his mouth down her neck and lower. Even though Bran had no claim on her. She'd said so herself. Royce's younger brother was planning to propose and she was planning on dumping him. What more evidence did Royce need that those two were ill-fated?

He pulled away and caught his breath, not knowing she'd robbed him of it until he greedily sucked in a lungful of oxygen.

Her eyes were wide and wild, her mouth opened to say... God, he had no idea... Everything about the kiss made him want to claim her for *himself.* To take what she was generously offering.

For once, practicality failed him. Against his better judgment he leaned in to cover her mouth with his for one more taste. Monday morning would come and he'd deal with consequences. But they didn't matter right now. What mattered was attraction. Set on simmer for years and now boiling over...

Just as he laid his lips on hers and pulled her flush against his body, the door at his back opened. They snapped apart like teenagers caught breaking the rules.

A breeze whooshed in from the force, sucking the air from the room, and judging from the look of panic on Taylor's face, every ounce of air from her body. She backed away from Royce a step.

Brannon stood in the doorway, his expression filled with surprise that faded into rage so fast Royce nearly missed the transition. "I sent you to find Taylor not make out with her."

"That's not—"

"I saw the light under the door," Bran said between clenched teeth. "And now I see the light in a different sense."

Royce had looked out for his siblings for as long as he could remember. He was the responsible one. It wasn't like he couldn't have physically stopped the kiss when Taylor advanced, he just…*hadn't*.

"It's my fault," he said, figuring she could blame him and save herself.

"Now I know why you discouraged me from proposing. So you could have her for yourself."

"Excuse me?" Taylor interrupted, offense radiating off her like her sweet perfume.

"I was going to propose to you tonight," Bran told her, his chin elevated.

"I know," she said. Gently. She was kind. Maybe too kind if she'd been dating his brother for her late father's sake more than her own. Why hadn't she had that pertinent discussion with Bran before tonight? If she'd let him down easy, he never would've purchased a ring.

And if she'd never seen the ring, the kiss never would've happened.

Which shouldn't have happened. But Royce was having trouble regretting it.

"You…knew?" Bran asked Taylor, his face turning an impressive shade of red.

"I saw you with the ring and I… I ran away. Royce

found me. I didn't mean to… I…I always wanted to kiss him."

"You did?" Royce and Bran asked at the same time. The brothers exchanged irritated glances.

"I planned on breaking up with you this weekend," she told Brannon, her focus solely on him. "In my head it was already done. I had no idea you were going to…" She gestured at his suit pocket where the telltale bulge of a velvet box confirmed his plans.

"I see." Embarrassment and a hefty dose of hurt outlined Bran's features before he turned to stalk down the corridor.

"Brannon, hang on." But before Royce could come up with some sort of suitable argument, Taylor touched his arm.

"Don't. This is my fault." She chased after Bran, moving as quickly as she could in her gown and heels. Royce leaned on the doorframe and watched her go. He slowly became aware of two women outside the ladies' room all but clutching their pearls. A member of the waitstaff had also witnessed the argument, but averted his gaze when Royce met his eyes.

Taylor caught up to Bran as he reached the exit and then they both walked outside. Royce rooted his feet to the floor. Taylor wasn't his. She never had been. And whatever had happened in this *Twilight Zone* slice of time never *should've* happened.

He'd been caught up in a moment—answering the call of attraction. One he hadn't known was there. He should've resisted. He knew better. His black-and-white worldview served a bigger purpose than simply ticking boxes on some cosmic checklist. Those rules and guidelines also kept the most important things where they belonged. In this case, kissing Taylor could shake the strong foundation of his very family tree. That had never happened before.

Nor would it, he vowed. Not on his watch.

Three

So, Saturday evening could've gone more smoothly.

The only explanation Taylor had come up with for the moment of insanity in the closet wasn't a pretty one. She'd kissed Royce because she wanted to. Simple as that. One opportunity and a little forced proximity was all it'd taken for her to fulfill the dormant fantasy. The kiss hadn't been thought out or rational. But since when was the heart rational?

Brannon Knox had nearly *proposed to her*. He'd taken first place for irrational!

As a result of her unplanned make-out sesh with Royce, the breakup with Brannon happened in the worst possible way. The kiss had put the final nail in that coffin. Actions speaking louder than words and all that. From the time her father declared Royce a no-go zone, Royce had taken up a certain amount of space in her world. He grew to be somehow bigger than life. Celebrity-like. Too far away to ever truly grasp. Which had amped up the attraction tenfold.

Royce had been inaccessible until that stray moment in private at the gala. She'd never been in his circle, not really, because he *was* older than her. Yes, they saw each other at work often and yes, they'd had meetings—even private meetings—but her professional side was every bit as rigid as Royce's. She'd never imagined a scenario that would lead to her kissing him in a coat closet. Kissing him ever.

Ugh. Slumping at her desk, she dropped her head into her hand. She wanted to die.

"Hiya, toots." Gia Knox, the younger sister of the two brothers who had been on Taylor's mind all morning, entered the corner office and shut the door. Taylor had gone to school with Gia—well, until college parted their paths. Taylor hadn't had the brains to land MIT, but few did. Bran hadn't been accepted. Royce hadn't wanted to go there, not that his father had minded. Jack had a streak of whimsy mixed in with his business acumen, like grenadine in Sprite, and had encouraged each of his children to follow their hearts.

"Good morning." Taylor kept her reply measured, not sure how her best friend felt about what had occurred Saturday. Taylor spent Sunday with her phone off, cleaning her apartment. As if that would purge any stray guilt.

"They're both duds if you ask me," the only Knox

daughter said with a wink. Her long dark hair spilled over the shoulders of a scarlet dress that kept her curves contained and professional. She was a Knox genius in Jennifer Lopez's body.

She was Taylor's closest friend and the one person she'd considered running to after stepping in it Saturday night. The last place she'd wanted to be was that ballroom in a sea of people, especially with Brannon. He'd been so angry... Justifiably.

That night when she'd followed him outside to explain, he'd spun on her, his voice sharp and unyielding.

"Royce, Taylor? Really?"

"Brannon, it wasn't—" She'd cut herself short of muttering a clichéd retort, though it was true. It really *wasn't* what it looked like. What it looked like was that she and Royce were sneaking off to make out in the closet. In reality Taylor's emotions had become tangled up in a rogue wave of attraction. "I never meant to hurt you."

From there the conversation had stalled, Bran's face dawning with the understanding that she'd seen the ring and fled. He hadn't stuck around to hear her reasoning for kissing Royce, which was probably for the best. What else was there to say?

"Do you hate me?" Taylor turned from her laptop to face Gia, who gave a blithe blink and dragged the guest chair closer to Taylor's desk. She sat, leveling Taylor with chocolate-brown eyes a touch darker than Royce's.

"I *adore* you." Gia offered a pitiable head shake.

"I had no idea Brannon was going to propose until he huffed back into the party snarling about how he'd made a mistake."

The blood rushed from Taylor's face. What had he told Gia? What had he told *everyone*?

Gia's hand covered hers. "I stepped out of the ballroom and into a private room with him, so don't worry about the gossip mill. Royce saw us and joined, and Bran gruffly admitted he'd made a mistake planning to propose at such a big affair. I had no idea he'd planned on asking you to marry him, Taylor. I thought you two were completely *caj*. Which I told him, by the way. Royce said he went to find you for *the Big Ask* but instead discovered you locked in the coat closet hyperventilating. Was it one-thing-led-to-another or is there more?"

The lump of dread in Taylor's throat remained, but she told her friend the truth. "I have no idea."

She'd been wondering that herself. Was the kiss the start of something? And if so, how could she navigate those choppy waters? Gia knew the truth and didn't hate her. Royce had greeted her this morning with a gruff "good morning" but he hadn't seemed upset. Was two out of three Knoxes *not* hating her enough?

"Are you okay?" Gia rubbed Taylor's knee.

Great question.

"I'm okay." Basically. "Brannon must hate me."

"His pride is hurt. But you don't have to guilt-accept a proposal."

Almost verbatim what Royce had told her. *You don't have to say yes to be polite.*

"Even if you did guilt-accept a few dates," Gia added.

Taylor watched her friend carefully. Gia had picked up on that on her own. When Taylor had started dating Bran, she felt like she'd crossed an unspoken boundary. How could she ask Gia's opinion or voice concerns over her best friend's flesh and blood? It would have been totally unfair.

"You don't miss a thing," Taylor told her.

"I was shocked when you walked into the gala together. I thought for sure he'd have a date and you'd come dance with me." She pressed her manicured fingernails into her décolletage and fluttered her lashes. "Honestly, I thought you two would've broken it off by now. I could see the distance. Or, well, not the distance so much as…the lack of spark."

"I was procrastinating. I care about him, just…not romantically. Not enough to marry him." She wondered if Gia would be this forgiving if she'd seen what Bran saw when he'd opened that closet door.

Spark City.

When Royce grabbed her up to kiss her for the second time, she'd been overcome. Laying one on him without any notice was one thing. Him reciprocating… That second kiss was heady. Consuming. Sparks zapped her like a free-swinging power line. They'd coursed through her bloodstream and lit up her brain like a neon sign. One that read *Royce Knox can kiss.* And boy, could he. She'd shared a few kisses with Bran over the course of their tepid dates, but none of them had measured up to the kiss in the closet with Royce.

That wasn't due to Brannon's lack of skill or personality. He was fun and made her laugh on a daily basis. He was distractingly handsome, with a dimple punctuating one cheek and a full, generous mouth. He had Royce's hard angles but there was an approachability to Bran that couldn't be denied. The Knox brothers came from good stock—both men were damned good-looking.

But. She'd never been *attracted* to Bran. He was an incredible friend. Or had been before she ruined their friendship with a spontaneous kiss.

If she could have a do-over, she'd have broken up with Bran a week ago—or maybe never would've said yes to that first dinner date. Hurting his pride at the beginning would have been better than at the end.

"I never saw that proposal coming," Taylor told Gia. "I assumed he'd lost interest. We were pretty much back to normal until the gala. He asked me to go with him and I didn't see the harm in it. You know how tedious these events can be."

"Lord, do I. So you two weren't..." Gia made a lewd gesture to indicate sex.

"No! God, no." Taylor couldn't help laughing.

"Hey, it's harder for me to hear than you, ladybug. If you ask me, this sounds like a big misunderstanding."

"I half expected him to politely break up with *me* by night's end." Though *hoped* might be a better word.

"And he would've been so nice about it," Gia said, which only served to make Taylor feel worse. "I'm not saying you weren't! Don't look at me like that."

"I panicked. I never in a million years thought he'd…" She shook her head, picturing the diamond ring in the box. Bran had been admiring the shimmer in the muted overhead light, his face… Wait. His *face*.

"He was looking at the ring right before I ran off. He… He wasn't smiling, Gia. He didn't look happy or excited. He looked… I don't know. Resigned?" And definitely not like a man in love.

"It really makes me wonder…" Gia let her thought taper off before pasting on a slightly insincere smile. "Never mind. Speculation is never good. Who knows what men are thinking?"

Taylor couldn't let her friend off the hook after that teaser. "*What?* What were you going to say?"

"Conjecture. And nothing that would help."

"It's not like you to be coy."

Gia chewed on her lip before she said, "I wonder if the proposal had anything to do with Dad's retirement. Pending retirement. Bran's being engaged would make him appear better suited for the role of CEO than Royce."

"He wouldn't?" But the sentence came out like a question because… *Would he?*

Brannon had mentioned time and again that his father would be stepping down. That he could picture himself in the role of CEO. Their "dates," for lack of a better word, had been consumed by talk of work and Bran's future at the company.

"Dad will retire sooner than we think, Tay," he'd told her one evening over a second glass of wine for each of them. He'd described Royce as his "competition." Bran had also mentioned that he wanted it more, but deserved it less. She'd argued in his defense that he and Royce were equally suited to replace Jack. It was the truth. The Knox boys each had winning qualities and were as dedicated to this company as they were to each other.

"I'm not saying he was using you, Taylor. I don't think he came up with an insidious plan to toy with you to get what he wanted."

"No, no, neither do I." Taylor had known Brannon practically her entire life. Ambition wouldn't cause him to stoop that low.

"But maybe somewhere down deep he thought it'd help to show some stability. Bran is the fun-loving one, after all."

"And president of the company. It's not like he's goofing around."

"Right. And you're COO. A match made in heaven, on paper." Gia tilted her head, her lips compressing. "Your dad always liked Bran for you."

He had.

"I couldn't live with myself if I drove a wedge between Bran and Royce." Taylor sighed.

"That's on them. You weren't the only one in that closet. Whatever amends need to be made, you'll work it out. What's done is done. There has to be a part of you that is glad you don't have to pretend with Brannon any longer."

"You're so understanding."

"Men are babies." Gia shrugged. "They'll get over it."

"I should talk to Bran." The idea of approaching him hung in the air like a foul stench. But they worked together, and closely. She didn't want there to be awkward vibes during meetings or conference calls. She didn't want him to avoid her out of discomfort or pride.

"You will. And you'll say something brilliant and then everything will be okay. He didn't act like a man in love, Taylor. I don't know why he thought an engagement was the right move, but he wasn't acting from the heart. It was pragmatism and planning if you ask me."

"I should've said what was on my mind that night. That we weren't working romantically. It would have been a relief for both of us."

"You should have," Gia agreed with a curt nod. "But you didn't. And now you have to make decisions starting from the square you're standing in."

A "square" was filled with Royce and her truckload of attraction to him. When she thought about him, apart from everything else, she had to admit it was exciting. Maybe she finally had a chance at a relationship that was visceral and real.

God, how she needed something real.

Even if she never kissed Royce again, she'd had a realization of sorts. She was still sexually attractive. After two years of no dating and her and Brannon's lackluster romance, Taylor had started wondering if she'd ever find someone who curled her toes.

She hadn't imagined that someone would be Royce. Years ago, she'd taken her father's warning at face value. He'd been protective over his baby girl when he'd told her to stay away from Royce. But she was a far cry from a baby now.

"See you in the quarterly meeting."

"Thanks, G."

"You're welcome, doll." Gia wiggled her fingers in a wave and left the office.

Four

Royce stepped into the financial review meeting, unbuttoned his suit jacket and took a seat at the sleek mahogany conference room table. As CFO, he'd be called upon for input but he wasn't running the meeting. That was up to the finance manager, Stella, who had already lined up the projector and was sifting through her notes.

He'd had trouble keeping his mind on work for obvious reasons. Work and play didn't mix. Not that he had time to *play*. Being in charge of the company's numbers was an undertaking he took very seriously.

Gia arrived last as per her usual. She sat next to Taylor, who was at Royce's left elbow. Brannon was across the table, leaning back in his leather chair, tapping a pencil eraser-side down while he glared in Royce's general direction.

Royce ignored him.

"Everyone ready to get started?" Stella asked rhetorically before doing just that. Meetings were a nuisance but necessary to keep everyone on the same page. Especially now that his father was flirting more and more with the idea of early retirement.

Jack Knox wouldn't hit the links right away nor was he interested in building birdhouses in his spare time. No, no. Jack planned on traveling, experiencing life and the world. Royce's old man, now sixty-one, had never truly run out of wild oats to sow.

Bran focused his attention on a paper report while Taylor and Royce consulted their tablets. Gia had a fussy leather notebook in front of her, bejeweled with gems and dotted with stickers. His baby sister wasn't much for formality. Brannon wasn't either, though he did follow along. He rarely used the very electronics their company sold, which made Royce laugh.

Or would have if Bran hadn't been shutting him out for two solid days.

The last conversation they'd had was at the threshold of that closet when Bran had caught Royce and Taylor post-lip-lock. When Royce had come upon Bran and Gia talking later that same night, Bran promptly turned and walked away. Royce understood his younger brother's anger. Seven unanswered text messages later, he'd given up, until this morning.

He'd stepped right into Brannon's corner office and addressed him with a "Good morning, brother."

Brannon had looked up from his laptop to narrow his eyes. Eyes that were lighter brown than Royce's own, and greenish like their mother's. He'd picked up his phone, made a call and started talking, ignoring Royce altogether.

That'd been two hours ago and here they sat, ignoring each other again.

With a sigh, Royce glanced at Gia, who was jotting notes and lounging in her chair at the same time. No doubt her big brain soaked up every word Stella was saying like a fresh, dry sponge. Gia had always been able to pay attention to everything around her. Bran was more easily distracted during boring moments like this meeting, while Royce enjoyed the methodology of a presentation. There was a certain order to it that made sense to him.

Jayson Cooper, Gia's ex-husband who still worked at ThomKnox, was notably absent from this meeting. Cooper was in charge of tech, but he'd sent his assistant, Whitney, to ferry back any pertinent information.

Taylor asked a question, drawing everyone's attention. Royce watched her openly, not a hardship since she was beautiful. He appreciated the way she'd come in today sans drama about Saturday night. She'd always been professional at the office, even though he remembered her differently when they were kids. She and Gia were about the same age, but Royce was six years older than the girls, and only a few years older than Bran. While Royce didn't exactly hang out with any of them when he was younger, social situations mashed them together.

Charity functions, raffles, art shows and galas like the Valentine's Day celebration on Saturday put them in fancy clothes at fancy affairs on the regular. Even when he was a gangly sixteen-year-old and she and Gia had been fifth graders. He hadn't thought of Taylor as more than his sister's friend, including when the girls were teens and attending those same functions in ball gowns.

As he'd aged up, so had Taylor. He could begrudgingly admit that her changes hadn't gone unnoticed. Charles Thompson's candid discussion about how Taylor wasn't a good romantic option for Royce had prompted no argument. Charles was like a second father and Royce respected the man immensely.

But since that very conversation, Royce had noticed attributes about Taylor that he hadn't previously. Physical ones, sure, but also the way she handled her life. She wanted everything and wanted it all at once. Like a kid at a buffet who agonized over how she'd fit a spoonful of everything onto the same plate.

Royce was simpler than that. He did better when his focus was narrow. Unfortunately for everyone, it'd been Taylor who'd narrowed his focus to a fine point on Saturday night.

No matter the reaction to a rogue kiss, the wisest course of action was to set them back on the path from which they'd strayed. They both cared greatly for ThomKnox, Taylor having been thrust into the position of COO after her father passed last fall.

It was a loss she took hard and he noted now, and not for the first time, that those feathered lines around her eyes were a new addition. Grief had taken a toll on Taylor and her mother, Deena, most of all. Jack Knox and Charles Thompson were best friends who didn't always see eye to eye but made the best decisions for the company. Since Charles's death, Jack had been less about the company and more about skydiving lessons, traveling to Africa for safari and scuba diving in the Great Barrier Reef.

His father might be having some sort of late midlife crisis, but Royce supported Jack's decision to retire, regardless of who was chosen for the CEO position. Both brothers wanted it. Bran had a knack for fusing fun and hard work and ending up with a blend both investors and employees enjoyed, so he was a valid choice. Probably the *better* choice.

Approachability was not Royce's strong suit. He was methodical and careful, prepared and concise.

Stella finished answering Taylor's question, and Taylor smiled, her bow-shaped pink lips forming the words *thank you.* Royce felt a pull from the center of his stomach down to his groin.

When Taylor grabbed hold of him and kissed him at the gala, he hadn't expected it. He'd only thought of her over the years as someone he *shouldn't* be kissing. Ever. That kiss had snapped his control in two and ushered in a loss of equilibrium that had changed his world.

Who wouldn't be tempted by that?

But temptation was a temporary dalliance. The moment had passed. He was determined to cram the meddling genie back into her glass bottle, wedge the cork and toss it out to sea. There was no room in a company about to lose their CEO and appoint a new one for squabbling between brothers. Especially over a woman as well respected as Taylor. She was in the upper echelon of ThomKnox. Investors liked stability. Nothing was more important than righting the already upset apple cart.

There was a certain order that Royce liked to keep and though change was inevitable, he preferred to get through it as quickly and painlessly as possible.

Taylor swept a lock of blond hair behind her ear, shifting in her chair so that one long leg slipped over the other. She circled her foot, wrapped in a tall black high heel and he allowed his eyes to trickle up a rounded calf to a supple thigh that vanished beneath the demure hemline of a black dress.

Stella's voice faded into background fuzz and his brain blurred in much the same way. It wasn't hard to admire Taylor before, but now that he'd had his lips on hers, he could easily imagine pressing those lush breasts to his chest and sampling her neck, smelling her soft perfume as he allowed the tip of his tongue to dip into her cleavage…

"Royce?"

By the sound of Stella's voice, that wasn't the first time she'd said his name. He jerked his attention to her, raking over Brannon's grouchy visage on the way. Stella smiled patiently. "The numbers you wanted to share?"

"Yes, thank you, Stella," he replied evenly. He flipped from one screen to the next on his tablet and pulled up the report, but the numbers stopped him cold. They were wrong. This wasn't…

Fantastic.

The report he'd queued up was from *last* quarter, not the careful one he'd been preparing for the bulk of the morning.

"Um… One second." Aware of every pair of eyes in the room on him, he opened a file in the Cloud and hoped to God he'd remembered to back it up there. Then he remembered he'd emailed it to both Brannon and Taylor. All he needed to do was pull up the sent email to access the correct report. He opened his mouth to tell Stella as much when Taylor spoke.

"I can take that question, Stella." Warm hazel eyes swept over him, almost slate gray against the backdrop of her black dress. "Royce and I were discussing that this morning, and there was some confusion as to who was presenting. It appears that the numbers for this quarter showed a nice increase going into next…"

Royce, rapt, listened as she smoothly read the numbers he'd crunched this morning, numbers he'd planned on presenting. He hadn't expected her to take over for him. But she had, sliding in and saving his ass as easily as she'd tugged his mouth down to hers last weekend. Impressed by her knowledge and ease with the topic, he couldn't tear his eyes off her for a solid minute.

When he did, it was only because he felt Brannon's gaze pinning him where he sat. Taking in his brother's ire was nothing new—there were plenty of times when they'd seen the world differently. Their father assured them that it was healthy for brothers to bicker, but Royce didn't think this situation was what Jack had in mind.

Locked in silent battle with Taylor between them, well... There was nothing healthy about it. It was bordering unhealthy. Royce could feel the animosity radiating off his brother and hoped to God no one else picked up on it.

He wouldn't stand for it.

Within ThomKnox were their careers—all of them. The entire Knox family's and Taylor Thompson's, too. His father was retiring soon and her father had left her with bigger shoes to fill as well. They were the next generation of ThomKnox. Time they started behaving like it.

Royce had never, to his memory, missed his cue in a financial meeting—in *any* meeting. The wild card that had changed everything?

Kissing Taylor Thompson.

The last intimate moment they'd ever share.

He had to put this behind him—for the sake of their future. His eyes clashed with Gia's and she quirked her lips in amusement as if saying *Something on your mind, big brother?*

Yes.

And he couldn't afford to have his mind anywhere other than work. The company was about to undergo a massive transition. Either Royce or Brannon would be CEO soon—they'd each been groomed.

The smoother the transition went, the sooner they could return to their regularly scheduled programming.

Royce glanced at Brannon, only this time he'd made a decision. He was going to have a conversation with his younger brother—whether Brannon wanted to or not.

Five

Taylor's mother's papillon, Rolf, stood on his hind legs and pawed Taylor's thigh.

"Such a beggar, honestly." She stroked the dog's fringed, butterfly-like ears.

"Don't feed him your—" Her mother clucked her tongue as Taylor handed over a cube of steak. Her mother was dressed for dinner in a pink skirt and suit jacket, a bumblebee-shaped broach pinned on the lapel and her matching gold jewelry shining. Her budgeproof lipstick was in place, her smooth, straight hair tucked behind one ear.

Deena Thompson fit into the role of wealth easily. Taylor's mother had been raised in a family of wealthy investors and business owners, most of her money hailing from the airline industry.

"He's a *dog*, Mother. He likes meat. Besides he enjoys beef more than me. I'm more interested in the potatoes and asparagus." Both of which she'd eaten already.

Dinner had been served rather formally in her mother's dining room. The table that stretched the length of the room was better suited for a packed Thanksgiving dinner, which her parents had hosted on numerous occasions, but this was where Deena Thompson liked to dine, so here they sat.

"He's a little dog, and I won't have him fat." Deena cocked her head to the side, sending her medium-length blond hair over one shoulder.

"One bite of steak won't hurt him, will it, Rolfie?" Taylor dropped her napkin on her plate and ruffled the dog's fur, nuzzling his tiny nose with her own. She'd never thought of a fussy toy breed like Rolf's as loving until her dad had been diagnosed. The little dog spent many, many evenings in either Taylor's or her mother's laps, soaking up their tears in his soft fur.

"He does love you," Deena said with a soft chuckle. "I think he believes you're his sister."

"Well. We both have great hair." Taylor gave her last cube of steak to the dog and ignored her mother's scoff.

Taylor was an only child but hadn't felt lonely growing up. She'd had her mother to pal around with, and the Knox siblings were a very big part of her world. Royce, Bran and Gia were raised by busy working parents as well as a team of nannies. Deena, while she'd always had a house staff, had been more than ready to leave the hectic working lifestyle to care for Taylor. Deena considered herself the ultimate domestic diva. She enjoyed keeping a house *and* a staff. She enjoyed catered dinners *and* selecting wines. She also enjoyed crafting in her massive craft room where every shade, pattern and color of scrapbooking paper lined the towering shelves on every wall. Now that Taylor thought about it, her mother's ambition at home *was* a career.

She was under no delusions that she had to mimic her mother's choices. Her work, which she loved, took up a lot of her time. Hiring help to clean her apartment was a no-brainer, especially when she spent her days as COO of a massive company. Sometimes though, she wondered how she'd balance work and family life once she decided to have a child of her own.

"Did you want more than one child?" Taylor scooted Rolf's front paws from her lap as her mother's chef stepped into the room to clear the plates. After they agreed everything was delicious and chose a dessert, he returned with two crème brûlées and tiny glasses of port wine.

Her mother dug into the crème brûlée, either ignoring or forgetting Taylor's earlier question.

"Mom?"

"Hmm? Oh, sorry. Children. We couldn't have any more." She shrugged, announcing it as easily as if she'd just run out of milk.

"What? You never…" Taylor shook her head in confusion while her mother sipped her port.

"No, no, not like that. Not like *couldn't*. Your father was busy with work and so was I. When the company expanded I wanted to hire my part out and stay home with my baby." She smiled warmly and patted Taylor's hand. "You."

"You never wanted to give me a brother or sister?"

"Well, we thought about it. But you had the Knox kids and I had my figure to consider." Deena winked, joking. She was beautiful for a woman of *any* age.

Taylor considered herself lucky to have inherited her mother's athletic build and love of exercise.

"What's bringing this about? Is a certain special relationship advancing? I never asked you about the gala."

Deena had attended for an hour or so before she made her exit. She told Taylor she'd felt inconvenienced by the idea of attending a party for show. Taylor couldn't blame her. Their grieving Charles's passing was a personal matter, and yet the masses felt they should be involved.

"You didn't hear about Brannon's proposal?"

"I didn't say I didn't hear about it. I said I never asked." Deena's eyebrows lifted.

"We broke up that night. Things at work are… strained. He's upset. Understandably."

"Well, you did kiss his brother."

"Mom! You know everything!"

"Patsy Sheffield told me," she said of their gossiping neighbor. "Your father wouldn't like that you're canoodling with the older Knox boy," Deena continued, the crème brûlée spoon hovering in front of her mouth. She cocked an eyebrow. "Did *you*? Like it?"

"He's hardly a boy, Mom." She could still feel the telltale scrape of his facial hair; see the dark look he'd given her before he gripped her waist and tugged her against his solid wall of a body. Taylor's cheeks warmed when she admitted, *"I liked it immensely."*

"Older men." Deena sighed. "There is something about them."

Deena was fifty-four years old, ten years Charles Thompson's junior. When she married Charles, who was selling and making a small fortune in direct sales at the time, Deena's father—Taylor's curmudgeonly but lovable grandfather—hit the roof. It was a story she'd heard time and time again as a little girl, told exuberantly by her father and interspersed with his infectious laughter at how he'd eventually won over his father-in-law. Her mother had laughed with him.

Taylor grew accustomed to the sound of her parents' comingling laughter. It'd stretched from her childhood until her father's passing last year, ending the only way it could—when he was no longer alive to contribute.

She'd recently been contemplating her father's reasoning behind her avoiding Royce. Even when he'd been very ill, he'd reiterated that Bran was a better fit for her and steered her away from the older Knox "boy."

"Well good for you for livening things up," her mother said. "Galas used to be fun, but now they're a drag. I only attended because it was the first time

I'd been out since…" She shook her head rather than say the words *your father's death*. "It's expected you show up and look like you're not in a million pieces."

"You're not. And it's remarkable." She reached for her mother's hand and Deena's eyes misted over. "I know you miss him. You must. I miss him like I lost a limb."

"Try losing all of them." Deena's mouth compressed into a tight line.

Dad had been less healthy than his wife—more into rich foods and cigars, and any activity that involved socializing. Taylor smiled a bittersweet smile at the memory of her father's warm personality. After losing him there'd been an absence of charm in her life.

There was a note of ease about Bran that reminded her of her dad, which likely had contributed to her agreeing to go out with him. But the attraction had been a big fat goose egg. If Bran would climb down off that high horse of his, he'd probably admit as much to her. When two people were attracted to each other they behaved like… Well, like Royce and Taylor had behaved in that closet.

Taylor had admired the Knox siblings her entire life—how close they were. She'd been treated like an unofficial sister. Jack and Macy were like a second set of parents. Royce, the oldest, hadn't been around much when Bran, Gia and Taylor were teens and he was in college. But whenever he returned to spend time with his family, Taylor noticed.

Until Saturday night, when Royce's hand had been

on her waist and his lips on hers, she wouldn't have guessed he'd *ever* notice her.

She recalled the silky softness on her fingers when she raked them into his hair. She'd wanted to climb that wall of masculinity to the summit. He'd been a perplexing mix of rigid and pliant during that kiss. Unraveling his straight-edged spine sent a zing of pleasure through her that hummed inside of her still. Had she seen him come unglued before last weekend? She didn't think so.

"I need to talk to Brannon," she told her mother. She'd been saying that a lot lately—to others and to herself. "Royce and Brannon were glaring at each other in a meeting today and I can't help thinking that's my fault."

Royce had been distracted in the financial meeting, and she'd bet she could also take credit for that. He'd been far from flustered, but when his eyebrows carved a deep line in his forehead, she'd read his expression as easily as she had his email. He needed help. So, she bailed him out.

"Brannon was out of line. You two are cute together, but marriage?" Deena shook her head. "I love that boy, I do. Don't get me wrong, I'm not saying Royce is the one for you, but darling, you're not married. You're certainly not engaged. You weren't anything when you shared that kiss except for curious."

And turned on, but that was too crass to mention.

"You're right."

"Perhaps the near-miss engagement is making you think about having a family. You're healing from losing your father. It's normal for your thoughts to turn inward."

"Coffee with the widow's group is helping." Taylor loved her mother but even Deena would be the first to admit that she'd never been what anyone would call "introspective."

"They're a lifeline. As far as your own future, don't pressure yourself. You love to do that, and I can tell you're trying to plot and plan. Let the future unfold on its own instead. See how that goes."

Easy for Deena to say. She loved to go with the flow. Taylor preferred *directing* the flow whenever possible.

"Who do you think Jack will name as his new CEO?" Deena propped her elbow on the table, wine in hand.

"Not Gia. She never wanted to run that company."

"Smart girl." Deena smirked. "I imagine it'll be Royce, don't you?"

"I could see either of them as CEO, but Royce's being older could be an advantage."

"Maybe Jack will name you."

"No." Taylor held out a hand like a stop sign. "I like my inherited position. It suits me. Plus, I like to think that I'm making Dad proud." She was going to say more but a lump in her throat stymied the words.

"Oh, honey." Her mother gave her a quick hug before bending over the table to address her quietly. "He's *so* proud. I know it. Charles always talked about how you're his legacy, Tay. You're like him in all the right ways. None of my underachiever tendencies. If you had a craft room filled with art supplies, you'd have a million-dollar business behind it. I just give them away." She smiled, though, knowing it wasn't a fault but simply the way she was. "When you're ready to start a family—no matter who you start one with—you'll succeed. Plenty of time for that, though."

"Thanks, Mom." Deena Thompson always said the right thing.

"I have a craft room to retire to and I know you're not interested in spending the entire evening with me. I suspect you have work to do even after eight o'clock?"

"You know me well." Taylor was looking forward to it, though. Her laptop was a comfort.

Her mother left the room, Rolf at her heels.

On the drive home, Taylor thought of Royce and what he was doing tonight. If he was home answering emails or tinkering with a spreadsheet. Had he thought of her since the kiss?

He would have had to... Wouldn't he?

Six

"I haven't thought about it, to be honest." Bran's cool expression was the opposite of the lethal one he'd worn when he'd opened that closet door at the gala. Royce guessed his brother would rather not have this conversation at all, but he hadn't left Bran much of a choice. Royce showed up at Bran's house without warning, walking in the second the door was opened.

Over bottles of beer, Royce began the conversation by stating the obvious. *We need to talk about Saturday night.*

Bran tipped his beer bottle against his lips and sucked down a few swallows.

Royce pulled his glasses off, having forgotten they were on his nose since he'd worn them the majority of the day, and tucked them into his jacket pocket.

"You've thought about it. I've thought about it. Don't bullshit me."

Bran scowled, the foreign expression now commonplace.

"You can't stay mad at us forever. It makes no sense. Taylor is COO, I'm CFO and you're the President."

"I know our roles."

"Soon one of us will be CEO." A hush fell over the kitchen. They were in direct competition for it, but fiercely loyal to one another. It was a new dynamic and one Royce wasn't sure how to navigate. He loved his brother but he also loved his father. If Jack assigned Royce the position of CEO, Royce would accept it. "You, Taylor, me. We're all integral parts of ThomKnox. If the investors get spooked—"

"*That's* what you're worried about?" Bran snorted, his smile condescending. "Jesus, Royce. I thought you were seducing Taylor in that closet. It's almost a relief to know you're still a cyborg."

"I wasn't seducing her." Anger pinged off his ribs like a pinball, but there was no sense in doing a postmortem. What was done was well and truly *done*. Royce would just say what he'd come here to say. "We're going to make it through this. We're family. But you have to have a conversation with Taylor that makes this okay. *You* were the one who nearly trotted out a proposal in a public place."

Bran's cheeks tinged red with embarrassment or anger—or a blend of both. He raked his hand through his longer hair and it fell every which way but back into place. "What the hell do you suggest I say to her, Royce? 'Sorry you found out I wanted to marry you?'"

"Did you *want* to marry her?" Royce held his brother's gaze, unrelenting. The proposal had been rushed, desperate. Definitely out of character.

"It doesn't matter now, does it?" Bran hedged.

"She panicked. She was practically hyperventilating stuck in that closet. When I found her, she had this wild, frightened look in her eyes and was muttering about how she'd never expected a proposal after only a few weeks of you two seeing each other." Royce lifted his own beer bottle. "She was hiding from you, Bran. Does that sound like a woman who would've responded well to your proposal?"

"Oh, so I should be thanking her for letting me down gently? Before I proposed and she publicly humiliated me?"

"Actually, yes."

Bracing his arms on the counter, Brannon's lip curled.

"The kiss was an accident."

"Looked pretty intentional to me."

It wasn't, but it had awakened Royce's dormant libido like the proverbial sleeping dragon. He worked constantly, content to be alone. If he needed a date for an event, he could find one—save the Valentine's Day gala. He'd run out of time.

The dates he took to a function rarely turned into

more. A few repeat dates, maybe. Sex sometimes—
he wasn't a masochist. But those dates were handled
as efficiently as everything else in his life. The ar-
guments were the same. He didn't have time to date.
Women took a lot of time.

See: the current situation.

"What I'm trying to say is that Taylor didn't mean
to kiss me."

"*She* kissed you?"

Dammit.

"Did you…enjoy it?" Bran's tone was curious.

"Of course not." Royce forgave himself for the
white lie he was about to tell. They needed to move
forward not dwell. "She apologized to me after. She
was flustered and embarrassed. I was selfishly glad
she admitted it first because I was about to do the
same thing. She's a good friend, a competent colleague."

"With a beautiful body and stunning mouth," Bran
muttered. But it wasn't jealousy that bent his eyebrows. It more resembled suspicion.

"I'm not blind to Taylor's attributes, but she's not
a good fit for me." Pragmatism was Royce's best ally.

Bran nodded, but looked like he had more to say.
Royce had said all he needed to say.

"Are we good?"

"Sure." Bran nodded. Royce didn't believe it was
that simple, but he'd take the reprieve.

"Talk to her." Royce shoved aside his barely
touched beer and stood from his seat at the counter.
"As her friend, you owe it to her to hear her out. And

if you're lucky, she'll let you explain your motives as well. Mistakes happen, Bran. Let's not allow them to cost us what's really important."

"Landing CEO?"

"May the best man win."

"Aw, shucks." Bran flattened his hand over his chest. "Do you mean it?"

Royce had to smile at his brother's cockiness.

"It's your birthright ahead of me, you know. That's not lost on me. Dad handing over CEO is like…the throne. You'd be crazy not to fight me for it."

"There's nothing to fight about. It's Dad's decision and I'll accept whomever he chooses. You're in the running. Throne or no." Royce bowed formally and added, "Your Majesty."

"You're an asshole. I bet Taylor regretted that kiss down to her size 9 Manolos." Bran grinned full out and Royce returned it, glad to be on the same page with him again.

"Without a doubt."

Royce had protected his family to the best of his ability and this was another situation where he'd do what was right. CEO was meant for him, but if Dad chose Bran, Royce would analyze spreadsheets and maintain the important role of CFO at ThomKnox for the rest of his days. Though being CEO would satisfy his own curiosity about what it would be like to step into his father's role at the company, he didn't need to prove anything to anyone.

As he walked out to his car, Royce looked through the window at his brother. Bran was leaning against the wall, his posture more relaxed than earlier, typing into his cell phone.

Hopefully that was Taylor he was texting. And hopefully she'd back up Royce's story about her regretting the kiss. Though he should probably prompt her in case she'd crafted a fictional tale of her own.

In the driver's seat, he fired off a few texts to her before starting the engine and leaving for home.

That ought to take care of everything.

Taylor stepped out of the shower, her hair wrapped in blue terry cloth, another blue towel wrapped at her waist. She'd stood in the steam for a long time to clear her mind. Tonight, rather than work her fool head off, maybe she'd relax. It'd be nice to shut off her work brain, watch TV or read a murder mystery instead of ruminate on Royce and Bran drama.

She used to be an avid dater, but when her father was diagnosed with cancer she put her social life on hold. Charles Thompson was enough man to occupy her time. Taylor didn't want to bring around a date who would meet her father when he wasn't feeling well—a date that might eventually attend a funeral as an awkward plus-one.

Bran had been a safe choice for reentry into the dating world. He'd gone to the funeral. He knew her father. There weren't any tough questions to answer or land mines to sidestep where her family was concerned. He understood her grief and sadness and during one date, when she'd told story after story about her dad, he'd smiled and listened.

Brannon was a good friend. And she hoped he would be again. She didn't like the unfinished business between them.

She took her time blow drying her hair and applying lotion to her arms and legs. She dressed in leggings and an off-the-shoulder long-sleeved T-shirt to thwart California's cool February evening. In front of the TV, she plopped down onto her reclining love seat. She grabbed her phone to turn it on silent before she chose a show to watch and noticed several text messages. One from Brannon. A few from Royce.

She swiped the screen and clicked on Brannon's name first. The text read:

We should talk about Saturday.

It was about time he came to the conclusion they'd have to speak eventually. She opened Royce's texts next.

I explained to Bran that you regretted kissing me and apologized immediately after.

You were panicked and confused. He'll understand.

As Taylor read the texts from Royce, her blood pressure slowly rose.

"I was confused? I *regretted* it?" she said through her teeth. Of all the… She stabbed the call button and lifted her cell phone to her ear. The second she heard Royce's smooth, neutral *hello* she let him have it.

"You told Brannon I kissed you and regretted it? You told him I apologized? To you? You told him I was confused!"

"That's the gist of it, yes."

She pulled in a breath through her flared nostrils. How, exactly, was this her problem? Like Gia said, Taylor wasn't the only one in that closet. "Did you regret it, Royce?"

He'd *clung* to her that night. Pulled her in and drank her kisses like his life depended on them. The way they fit together, even in their formalwear, suggested they'd fit together a whole lot better wearing a whole lot less.

"Of course I regretted it," he answered in the same bland tone.

"No you didn't." He might have shown zero interest in her before that fated closet run-in but not so now. She'd witnessed him taking a painfully slow perusal of her from head to toe in the financial review meeting. "You brought the wrong report to the financial review."

"Thanks for the reminder of my incompetence." He sounded peeved, which peeved her. He wasn't upset about the kiss, but oh-ho! He brought the wrong report! Scandal!

"You seemed distracted at the meeting," she reminded him. "Was there something—" *or someone*

"—keeping you from thinking clearly that morning, Royce?"

"Yes." His low growl of affirmation sent her heart into a twirl. She knew it. She knew there was more to that kiss than proximity. "It won't happen again."

It was less of a promise and more an assertion. How could he be so sure? *She* wasn't sure. She stopped shy of blurting, *You looked like you wanted to lick my legs from Achilles to inner thigh.*

An involuntary shudder shimmied up her spine as she imagined Royce's mouth on her legs. His tongue climbing her leg, tickling behind her knee before going higher. It was bad enough she knew what his lips felt like on hers. It'd only made her want more.

Speaking of…

"Did you mention to Bran that after I *threw myself at you* in a fit of 'panic' and 'confusion' that you swept your tongue along mine until neither of us could think straight?" Heart thudding heavily, she waited. He didn't respond right away, which made her feel smug. She was absolutely right about the effect of that kiss. It'd surprised both of them in the best way possible.

"I was carried away," he murmured.

Satisfied, she smiled as she brushed her hand along the soft suede arm of the love seat. So she had rocked his world. *Not bad, Tay.*

"ThomKnox is facing a very big transition in the coming weeks and months after my father retires. As top brass, our focus needs to be on our shareholders and investors. You don't have to worry about my mouth on yours—on any part of you—again. We can continue at work the way we have in the past. I trust you agree that it's best we appear as one cohesive management team."

The shift from such a personal comment to words as impassioned as a cardboard cutout pissed her off. Royce valued control. This much she knew. But acting like another kiss might disturb the otherwise perfect harmony at ThomKnox? Come on. How cocksure could one man be?

Denying the real attraction that existed between them wasn't only a fabrication, it was cruel. She hadn't had a man in her bed for nearly two years. Two years! She'd put her attraction, her desire for another person, on hold. She'd funneled every ounce of her remaining energy into prayers and good vibes and meditation and research on alternate medicines for her father. Anything to give him another year—another twenty years—on this planet.

None of her efforts had changed what fate had so cruelly set in motion. Her father was destined to die no matter what she did to stop it. It was unfair, and she'd wailed those words at the blank white ceiling of her bedroom on more than one occasion. And now Royce thought he'd come along and *mansplain* away how she was feeling when she kissed him? And worse—claim he hadn't felt the attraction she damned well knew was there.

What a load of crap.

"You can lie to me about that kiss," she told him, "but you know the truth deep inside."

"The truth, deep or otherwise, is that it shouldn't have happened. I'm willing to forget it, and I suggest you do the same."

Seven

After Taylor ended the call with Royce—hanging up on him as he deserved—she didn't have the energy to confront Brannon. First, she was too angry with the eldest Knox brother and didn't want to take it out on the wrong one. Second, and as much as she hated to admit it, Royce was right.

The company was facing a very big transition and it was of the utmost importance that the top brass were one cohesive unit. She and Brannon had both made mistakes. Him, planning a proposal when they'd never so much as slept together and her, not breaking up with him when she knew damn well their relationship hadn't stalled—it never started.

That saying about eating crow swooped by on wide black wings, her father's sage voice echoing in her ears. *If you have to eat crow, might as well do it while it's warm.*

In other words: no more delaying doing the right thing.

She purposefully came in late the next morning to avoid chitchat and the possibility of bumping into Brannon or Royce on the way to her office. The executive suites had some distance between them in the sprawling building. At least she could ensure privacy for her conversation with Brannon.

After checking their shared meeting calendar and determining he was in, she straightened the skirt of her slate-gray wrap dress and headed to Bran's office.

His personal assistant, Addison Abrams, had worked for ThomKnox since last June and was, according to Brannon, indispensable. She was smart, attentive, and as far as Taylor knew, incredibly kind. Addi was one of the first people in the office to approach her after her dad's death, both with kind words and a touch to the arm that had turned into a gentle hug. Taylor would never forget that small but meaningful gesture.

"Good morning." Taylor checked her slender wristwatch before correcting with a smile, "Late morning."

"It's still morning." Addi's smile was cooler than usual. Typically, she was quick to compliment Taylor on her wardrobe. Maybe gray wasn't Addi's favorite color. The two women didn't converse outside of ThomKnox, but Taylor wouldn't have been surprised if she and Addison someday formed a friendship. "What can I do for you, Ms. Thompson?"

The formality was new, too.

"Everything okay?" Taylor ventured.

Addi's platinum blonde hair was a few shades lighter than Taylor's and wound into a twist at the back of her head. Addi's dress was a bright, sunset orange and would've been appalling on any other woman. But with her high cheekbones, ocean-blue eyes and golden skin tone, Addison was a true Cali girl. The vivid color suited her.

Those blue eyes were icy when she responded, "Everything is fine."

Oh-kay. So much for small talk.

"I'm dropping in on Bran if he's not busy. Is he on a call?" Taylor asked.

The other blonde checked the desk phone where a red light blinked twice before vanishing. Addi sounded inconvenienced when she announced, "Not anymore."

"Perfect. I'll let myself in?"

Addison nodded, her smile forced.

Taylor rapped lightly on Bran's office door before letting herself in. She'd caught the expression of surprise on his raised face through the slatted wood blinds just before she entered. "I'm responding to your text finally."

"In person, no less." He didn't wear a scowl as well as Royce. Bran was better suited for a smile or a mischievous smirk. "Have a seat."

He gestured to the pair of dark leather chairs in front of a glass coffee table and stood to join her. Before he left his desk, he pressed a button on his phone and spoke into it. "Addison, can you send in an intern with drinks..." He let go of the intercom button to ask Taylor, "Is it too early for a drink?"

"Coffee will do."

He dipped his head and pressed the intercom button again. "Coffee. Black for her—"

"Cream and two sugars for you," Addi finished. "I'll arrange it." Her voice was warm when she addressed him. Interesting.

"So Addison isn't unhappy in general, only with me."

Bran didn't deny it. "More like misguided protection. She works for me which means she's automatically on my side."

Addi sent a withering glare through the blinds before stalking off. Taylor wasn't sure Bran had that right. Addi didn't like that Taylor was in Bran's office. With the door shut. Probably she'd heard about the failed proposal and the kiss. Who knew what sort of rumors had been flying around the office?

Bran had already taken his suit jacket off—it was a rare occasion that he wore it—but his tie was knotted at his neck. It was a fun design—yellow with bright orange suns. Taylor had the passing thought that it complemented Addison's dress.

They shared pleasantries about a few emails that had come through regarding a new laptop design until an intern arrived with a tray. The conversation was slightly forced, and given Brannon's stilted responses, he felt the same way. There seemed to be an unspoken rule about civility that almost gave Taylor pause.

Almost.

Bran poured her a cup of black coffee, doctored his own with too much cream and sugar and leaned back in the chair, mug in hand. He was waiting for her to speak, and why shouldn't he? She'd come to him.

"Why do you want to marry me?"

He blew out a soft chuckle. "I don't."

"You *did*," she replied calmly.

"I..." He shook his head, frowning to himself. "Clearly, it was a mistake."

"We hadn't been on an official date in at least a week. And the chemistry wasn't exactly sizzling those two times we kissed."

"Thanks a lot."

"Bran," she said through a laugh. "I'm one of your best friends. Be honest with me."

He stared down at his coffee for several beats before meeting her gaze. "The kisses could have been better. But. That wasn't my fault."

"And you thought an engagement would improve our odds?"

He set down his mug and leaned forward, elbows on his knees. "Engagements can last a long time. How do you know?"

There was something he wasn't saying. Him being coy was getting them nowhere. Gia's comment about Brannon looking like a better option for CEO made sense. And Taylor, despite coming in here to extend an olive branch, couldn't do it knowing that she was nearly proposed to out of convenience.

"Royce lied to you."

Brannon frowned.

"I didn't apologize to him after kissing him. And while I regret the timing—I absolutely should have ended things between you and me a few weeks ago after that awful seafood dinner."

Bran's eyebrows jumped. "We've never had that difficult a time trying to hold a conversation."

"Never," she agreed. "You can tell me why, you know. I *am* your friend."

She balled up her fist and slugged him in the arm. He smiled that cute Brannon smile she'd admired for as long as she'd known him. It might not light her up the way Royce's did, but Bran was still ridiculously attractive.

"CEO means a lot to me. This company means a lot to me. I want a family and kids, but I thought I'd have that before my role at the company changed. Now that it's a one out of two possibility, I felt like…" He shrugged. "I should get the ball rolling?"

He winced, probably not liking how that sounded out loud. But she knew him—had known him her whole life. Gia was right. He hadn't used her. He'd been caught up in the race for CEO.

"So your ambition was in the lead. Admit it. You don't want to marry me."

"It was too soon," he said instead, probably trying to spare her feelings. He might've been blowing by her like a stiff wind lately, but face-to-face, he couldn't be unkind.

"For the record, I don't think you did it on purpose. Your heart is as big and inclusive as your father's.

You'd do anything for your family, for this company. Even something as misguided as marriage."

He put his hand to his forehead. "God, Taylor. What *was* I thinking?"

"I should have walked up to you when you were holding that ring and asked what it was." She shrugged. "Instead...I panicked."

Crap. She *had* panicked. One point for Royce.

"And locked yourself in a closet."

"That was an accident."

"Was the kiss an accident?" Bran looked genuinely curious. "You and Royce..." He shook his head. "You two are more mismatched than you and me."

"Well, we both drink white wine and you won't touch it, so we have that going for us."

"Your father proposed to your mother at that gala. And you've been sad. I thought—hell, I don't know what I thought. It was the wrong thing to do."

"So your heart was involved after all," she said gently. He was sweet. No matter what reasoning was behind the doomed proposal.

He stood, taking her hands and helping her to her feet. "Friends?"

"Always."

He pulled her into a hug. When she dropped her arms, he wore his usual mischievous grin. "Damn. That was an awful hug. Dare I say...*disgusting.*"

"Appalling," she teased back. She lifted her mug to take one more sip of her coffee when she caught a flash of bright orange at the window. Addison's mouth was a compressed line, her gaze hard. And hurt.

"There's someone out there for you, Taylor," Bran said. "But not me. Now stop begging me to go out with you. It's embarrassing."

"In your dreams, buddy."

"It's not Royce, either."

"What makes you say that?" She wasn't going to deny there'd been something in that kiss. Something unexpected. Something worth pursuing.

"I don't want to see you hurt. As your *friend*, I'm saying you can do better."

She nodded, hoping that the nod communicated that she agreed. She couldn't exactly *disagree*. Royce had been a pompous ass lately.

"Thanks for stopping by." Brannon opened his office door. Then to Addison he said, "Taylor can't keep her hands off me."

The joke did *not* go over well. Taylor walked away feeling Addison's eyes on her back the entire time.

Jealous much?

She wanted to go back and comfort Addi, to tell her there was nothing going on with Brannon, and there never had been. But she couldn't right that relationship before she fixed another one…

With ThomKnox's stubborn CFO.

Eight

Everything was back to normal by the end of the week.

Sort of.

Royce had been mesmerized by numbers and reports come Friday morning until Taylor marched in, arms flying. And he did mean *marched*.

She'd come in to complain about Lowell Olson—the owner of Box, an elite electronics store. Lowell was in discussions about where and how to shelf ThomKnox products—something Box had never done before.

"Apple is not the only sleek, sexy product on the market, you know. We have a good—no, *better*—tablet right around the corner and he acts like we should pay him double what they're paying for premium shelving!" While Taylor talked, one of the pearl buttons on her silk shirt wiggled loose.

Royce tried to reroute his eyes—honest to God—but they kept flitting back down to that gap showing a swatch of pale pink bra. His body tightened, the memory of the kiss slamming into his gut like a two-by-four. Finally, he looked down at the tablet in front of him and pretended to read the notes he'd taken at yesterday's meeting.

"Are you listening to me?"

He repeated her last sentence back to her. "'Lowell is a buffoon if he thinks ThomKnox can't stand up to any brand on the market. And his company's bottom line is as tiny as his prehistoric brain.'"

She bit her bottom lip, trying to hide a smile. That attraction he'd been trying to ignore? Wasn't working. She'd been carrying on as usual. He'd been barricaded in his office, only attending meetings he was required to attend simply to let the—*whatever* was between them—pass. It would. He'd see to it.

"Was I close?" he asked.

"Spot-on. It sounded funny in your serious tone."

"I'm one-note. Can't help it." His eyes strayed to her shirt again and the bra playing peekaboo.

"You are not." Her smile suggested she saw him differently than a rigid numbers guy. It was oddly appealing.

"Are you looking at my shirt?"

"No." He averted his eyes.

"Royce! You could have told me I was flashing you." She quickly fixed the open button.

"I didn't want you to think I was harassing you at your place of business. You are a colleague and I respect you."

She flipped her hair over her shoulder. "Well, the next time my breasts are on display, or any other body part, please tell me."

He frowned. Mainly because now all he was thinking about was what the rest of her would look like on display.

"Okay."

"Anyway. Hopefully Lowell will come around before the new tablet launches. We need as many eyeballs on it as possible." She pointed to the interoffice mailer she'd dropped in his inbox when she'd walked in. "Can you sign that really fast?"

"What is it?" he asked, opening the envelope.

"Birthday card for Addison."

"Could you have chosen one with more glitter?" He brushed the stray gold specks from his desk before scribbling his name into the card and handing it back to her. "Is there a reason you're taking her card around personally?"

"I need to run off the steam that built after the interaction with Lowell."

"It'll work out."

"I'm also seeing to it that Addison receives her birthday card from me personally." Taylor took the envelope. "As a gesture of goodwill. Well, this and a giant bouquet of Please Stop Hating Me flowers."

"Addison doesn't hate you. She likes everyone." She was bright and smiley and professional. Bran wouldn't shut up about what an amazing assistant she was whenever he mentioned her. Which was usually when Bran was trying to talk Royce into hiring an assistant of his own on a permanent basis. Royce utilized the interns for delegation. A personal assistant seemed too…in his space.

"She shot daggers at me through Bran's office window when she saw me hug him." Eyes rolling to the ceiling, Taylor missed Royce's reaction. He went stock-still, his fist choking the life out of the gold-and-black Mont Blanc pen in his grip.

"You what?"

"I talked to Bran." She dismissed the topic with a hand, like news of *the hug* wasn't a bombshell shaking the walls of Royce's skull. "Addison saw us and I don't think she liked it."

Well. That made two of them.

"I think she likes him, but he's too thickheaded to notice."

"Why were you *hugging* Brannon at all?" The question came out like a thunderclap. He rolled his shoulders and fingered his bow tie, trying to calm down.

"Because Brannon's my friend?" She looked at him like he'd gone crazy, and hell, maybe he had. She'd hugged Brannon before. She'd hugged *Royce* before—he thought. He seemed to remember a few stiff-armed side squeezes over the years. But if Addison was jealous…

"That must've been some kind of hug."

She watched him carefully. A little too carefully.

"I have a lot to go over here—" he gestured to his tablet "—if you don't mind."

Still skewering him with a look, she reached up to finger the button on her blouse, drawing his attention to the silk shirt that touched her body like a caress.

He imagined undoing each of those pearl buttons and sliding the blouse from her skin while covering every revealed inch with his mouth...

"Thanks for the signature," was all she said.

He blinked, snapping his eyes to hers. In a voice of steel, he said, "No problem."

She left and he sagged in his chair. Categorizing Taylor as his coworker and family friend wasn't working. Especially when she was impassioned. Worked up over Lowell or insisting Addison like her again—both made her more tempting.

Royce couldn't allow himself to be tempted. He had to work—and focus on the company's naming a new CEO. Turned out after his lecture about being responsible, Taylor had taken his advice and smoothed out the issue with Bran. He should be glad.

So why wasn't he?

Royce left the office earlier than his usual six o'clock. His father, Jack, had requested he join him at Rust and Boar, a steakhouse known for its elitist lounge. Fine by Royce. He couldn't concentrate on a damn thing anyway.

Usually over cigars or brandy, or both, Jack Knox made the deals he'd become famous for—the same ones that'd made ThomKnox billions. Jack wasn't one for cigar smoking, though. That'd been Taylor's father Charles's passion more than Jack's. Jack held tight to tradition, however, and liked that even in California, where it rained granola, they could still discuss business over a slab of meat and a stiff drink.

Royce smiled to himself as he recalled the last business meeting that went down in Rust and Boar, mainly because Taylor had come in her father's place. She'd done her father proud. ThomKnox was not and never would be a boys' club. Taylor was as respected—if not more respected—than any man in the company.

He frowned when he thought of how much he liked that about her. How it made her tantalizing in a way other than physically. A woman he should be admiring from afar for her stellar work ethics had somehow worked her way under his skin. It didn't match his ethos and that was possibly more disturbing than anything. Royce was always in control. For Taylor to pop him at the seams... It made no sense.

Stress. He could blame stress. The possibility of being named CEO was a big deal. Brannon and Royce not getting along for a few days was a big deal. Lowell Olsen was a thorn in their sides.

Yes. Blaming stress would work fine.

Not calling himself on his own BS, he stepped inside the restaurant. He spotted his father at the bar, white head tossed back and laughing heartily with the woman next to him. The woman was a very big part of ThomKnox's success and Royce's first love: his mother, Macy.

"Royce!" She threw her arms up when she saw him.

He came close and kissed her cheek. "You're looking beautiful this evening." Then he turned to shake his father's hand. "Dad. Good to see you."

"Our table is being prepared." Jack grinned, his smile bright and genuine. Brannon definitely had that side of Jack—the lighter, more infectious side. Royce had inherited his dad's cunning instincts and head for business.

Can't win 'em all. Besides. Royce was better at rigid and unapproachable. Call it an art.

"Mr. and Mrs. Knox, your room is ready." A suited man, black leather menu boards in the crook of one arm, turned to lead them from the bar to a private window-filled room. Nicknamed "the sun room," the upstairs private room actually belonged to Thom-Knox and was often used for special occasions. Royce assumed it'd be where they held his father's retirement party. If Jack ever got around to announcing it.

"What's the occasion?" he asked his parents once they were seated by the window, a breathtaking view of mountains and blue skies in the backdrop. It was rare to have dinner just the three of them. Usually Bran, Gia and, when they were married, Jayson Cooper, were present as well.

"Wine first. Then we'll discuss." Decree made, Jack took his time tasting different vintages before settling on a bottle for the table. They ordered the chef's special of almond-crusted rainbow trout with wilted greens and were halfway through their dinners when Jack was suddenly ready to talk.

"I'm naming you CEO." He made the announcement without fanfare, after forking a bite of trout and chewing thoughtfully.

Royce, napkin in hand, slowly lowered it to his lap and exchanged glances with his mother. Her genial smile suggested she knew what was coming and approved of the decision.

"An announcement will be at the office. I'll hold a meeting and we'll make it official. I wanted you to be prepared. Give you some time to digest the news. I know you're slower to accept change than Bran or Gia."

"Do they know?"

"They will soon," answered his dad.

"Gia doesn't want CEO," his mother chimed in. "She never has. She has aspirations. If you ask me, they're not in marketing. She had to move somewhere after hers and Jayson's divorce."

"Mark my words," Jack said, "she wants to take over the technology department."

"Coop will love that," Royce muttered under his breath. Jayson Cooper wasn't above being ruled by a female, but his ex-wife was next level.

"Brannon wants CEO. And we know that," his mother said.

"But you want it more," his father said.

Royce shook his head, but it was for show. Everything in him leaned forward as if shouting YES. Jack raised a hand to stay anything to the contrary Royce might've said.

"You deny yourself what you truly want. You always have. You're our ambitious firstborn and yet so ready to sacrifice for your siblings," Jack said with a proud smile. "But you can't deny you want this. You're ready."

"It's our way of saying that it's past time to say yes to yourself," Macy added.

"It's also completely selfish." Jack placed his fork and knife on his plate. "You're the one who should be running ThomKnox, no one else. You're the one who can level up with the company. I'm going to be busy building a private resort on an island for your mother and myself to vacation. No time or desire to care about the future of ThomKnox." His father winked to show he was exaggerating.

Hearing the words "no time or desire to care" made Royce's shoulders draw back in pride. He *did* care. He *had* the time. Since graduating high school and doggedly pursuing a college degree he'd been invested in ThomKnox. Not to say that Bran didn't love his family or the business—he did, and so did Gia. But this was about what was right for the company. Who would be more dedicated, more available. That person was obviously Royce.

He wasn't encumbered with a wife or a girlfriend. And now that this was almost settled, there would be no limbo. He could move forward and put the snafu between him and Taylor behind him.

He wanted CEO. Down to his very marrow.

Jack let out a soft chuckle and patted his son's cheek like he had when Royce was a kid.

"There he is," Jack said to his wife. "Told you he'd love it."

Macy nodded. "Yes. You did."

Only then did Royce allow himself to grin. To feel the buzz of satisfaction throughout his entire body.

CEO was his.

He would make his parents proud.

Nine

Taylor hung her silk shirt in the closet and fingered the delicate fabric, her mind on Royce. He'd been checking her out today. His not mentioning her popped button had nothing to do with *respecting her as a coworker*. What was it with men and their complete denial of what was right in front of them?

She shook her head. It'd been a long day. Best not to analyze that stumper. She stripped off her slacks and hung them as well, sliding one hanger then another to the side in search of her favorite pair of comfy leggings.

What was Royce trying to prove today? That she was objectively unattractive? She swiped another hanger, remembering the moment she'd caught him looking. *Really* looking.

"Eating me up with those deep brown eyes…" And then denying it.

Vehemently.

"What's he afraid of?" she asked her closet.

What are you *afraid of?*

Valid point. Why hadn't she called him on it? Why hadn't she confronted him the way she had Bran? Was it propriety? Was it procrastination? Or was it some latent, misplaced loyalty to her father's wishes?

Ding! We have a winner!

It wasn't like her to not go after what she wanted. Until now, however, Royce had never given her a reason to pursue him. He'd never looked at her the way he'd looked at her today. It'd been exhilarating watching him at war with himself, the silent battle pulling the sides of his mouth into a frown. It was as if he'd been giving himself a stern talking-to. Worse, she'd let him off the hook. All because her father had once suggested that Royce was not the man for her. At the time, she'd found it funny. Royce hardly gave her a passing glance.

"Today, it was more than a passing one."

She really needed to get a cat. Or a goldfish. Muttering to herself alone in her apartment was a recipe for a straitjacket. She slid another hanger and encountered a garment she'd forgotten about.

Seth Wheeler had been a longish term boyfriend for Taylor. They'd nearly made it to a one-year anniversary, and she'd believed they might even get married and have a family someday. Her parents liked him and Taylor herself felt stirrings of love after only a month. When Seth finally uttered those three words to her, she'd happily returned them. They were together but separate people, both busy professionals who prioritized their careers. Then Seth, an engineer, had been offered an opportunity in Dubai the very same day Taylor had learned of her father's cancer diagnosis.

Her life abruptly changed for the worse. In so many ways.

Seth was ecstatic about the "once in a lifetime opportunity." He was also unwilling to stay in California. Taylor refused to leave her father's side. She'd expected Seth to turn down Dubai. To stay here with her while her father fought for his life.

Seth instead left her behind. He'd been apologetic but oh-so-selfish. "What's between us, Tay, it may not work out long-term," he'd told her. "But Dubai? It's a sure thing."

Mind returning from the past, she fingered the delicate lingerie. She'd purchased the luxurious La Perla slip specifically for her and Seth's one-year anniversary. The black slip sailed over her body like a whisper, making her feel undeniably feminine. The hand-embroidered floral design framing the neckline and the low V-shaped dip in the back made the piece a work of art.

And since she bought it for the way it made her feel, not because Seth would've liked it, she kept it. She told herself that someday there'd be another man in her life who would make her want to slide into the seven-hundred-dollar garment.

As she rubbed the silky material between her fingers, she thought of Royce's reaction to hearing the news that she'd talked to, and hugged, Brannon. Royce had looked like he wanted a few carpenter's nails to gnaw on. She'd bet he was suffering from the same green-eyed monster as Addison.

Royce was *jealous*.

"Like silk, do you?" She pulled down the black velvet hanger, a positively delicious idea popping into her mind. Maybe it was time—past time—to challenge her father's opinion about whom she should or shouldn't date. She loved her father. She respected him. Her dad had the best intentions when it came to her. But he also could've been *wrong*.

Royce wanted her. She wanted him.

What more did she need to do?

Prove it. That's what.

The flirty short skirt showcased her toned thighs. The skinny straps framed her shoulders. The boldness of showing up unannounced wearing it would be Royce's ultimate weakness. No way could he deny his attraction then.

It was past time she did something because *she* wanted to do it. Not what her parents wanted. Not what her friends wanted. She'd been dating the wrong guy in some misguided effort to please her father, for heaven's sake. Enough was enough.

Sparks didn't come along every day. And the ones that flew between her and Royce were so rare, she couldn't remember the last time she'd felt anything like it. Not even with Seth.

She unearthed a snow-white, thigh-length trench coat next, and from the shoebox on the top shelf of her closet, pulled down her highest black heels. The little ankle straps would go nicely with the acres of leg showing beneath the coat.

Wearing only a mischievous smile, she climbed into a warm shower for a quick rinse. Twenty minutes later she was in her car driving to Royce's house.

Uninvited.

Royce arrived home and tossed his key fob into the decorative bowl in the foyer. A lush green plant sat next to the tall narrow table in the entryway, its leaves shined to glossy perfection by his housekeeper. She also left a bowl of lemons on the kitchen counter along with a vase of fresh flowers in the dining room.

He appreciated those kinds of details. Living alone was fine with him, but he liked life breathed into the space that he returned to each day after work. It gave him a sense of not being alone, but he was never required to converse. Which he also liked.

At least he *usually* liked it.

Since his parents had shared the news that he was CEO, Royce had been elated. Practically buoyant. Talk about two emotions he didn't feel often, if ever. His mother had taken a car home and he and his father retired to the bar for a scotch. Jack had reiterated that he would tell Gia and Bran personally, asking Royce not to say anything of their clandestine dinner. "Rumors can destroy a company," he'd warned.

Didn't Royce know it.

"You're brilliant," his father had added. "Hell, all my children are. But you are thoughtful and slow to speak. Careful in the right ways. That is what will make you a great CEO."

Royce had agreed with that assessment. Then his father said something that made Royce frown.

"You're also careful in the wrong ways. Being reckless is okay from time to time. The world won't come off its axis if you do something wild."

His mind arrowed back to—who else? Taylor Thompson. The kiss in the closet that never should have happened. It had been wild. Barely restrained. And while the world wasn't knocked from its axis, it had been given a solid shove.

Taylor was an indulgence. An indulgence he was supposed to have forgotten about by now. An indulgence that should've been satisfied a week ago. An indulgence that was making him itch like he was wearing a new wool sweater. He needed to do *something*, but he had no idea what.

He tossed his jacket onto the back of the dining room chair and removed his cuff links. He didn't typically undress in his kitchen but before he did anything else tonight, he was celebrating. A glass of wine would be nice. Then he could toast to himself.

He bent to pull a bottle of Old Vine Zinfandel from its home in the wine rack and admired the sleek black bottle with the pewter emblem on the neck. His house, normally welcoming and quiet, felt like a soundproof cocoon. He was happy but had no one to celebrate with—he couldn't call up Gia or Bran—so he was stuck with his own company.

Keeping secrets from his siblings didn't sit well with him, though he understood his parents' motivations. They needed to tell Gia and Bran in their own time and in their own way. Royce respected that. He opened the bottle and poured a few inches of the red into a wineglass.

Unsure what to do with himself, he flipped on a table lamp and sat on the new-but-made-to-look-worn leather sofa. Strumming his fingers on his knees, he spotted the remote for the fireplace. In the click of a button flames flickered to life. Wine in hand, he sipped, struck by how odd it was to sit here without work in front of him. He set the wineglass aside, lifted a magazine off the table, also left in place by his housekeeper, and idly flipped through it before setting it aside as well.

He grunted what might've been a laugh. His father was right. Royce really *didn't* know how to unwind.

The doorbell chimed and he jumped off the couch, almost embarrassingly eager to invite whomever it was inside. Even if it was one of his siblings, he could still share a glass of wine if not the reason behind it. Shared wine with company was a hell of a lot better than sitting here alone.

The black-and-white security screen in the kitchen showed a woman standing on his front porch but she was too tall to be Gia. He leaned in for a closer look.

"Taylor?" His first thought was that something awful had happened. Why else would she stop by unannounced? His second thought, after he'd yanked the door open, was that she was at the *wrong* house.

Her tiny trench coat was belted in the middle and hiding what he guessed was a very short dress. Her legs were smooth and tan, ending in a tall, spiked pair of heels. Her hair was slightly wavy, the same way it'd looked at the office except…bouncier.

Turned out he'd have someone to celebrate with after all.

Be practical. Practicality came as naturally as breathing for him.

But it wasn't easy to be practical with Taylor in front of him looking like sex in stilettos. She teetered, those tall spindles nestled in the crooks of his cobblestone porch. The shoes were black and wrapped enticingly around her ankles with delicate straps and tiny gold buckles. Those delicate straps led to shapely calves, cute knees and up, up to a pair of plush thighs.

An eager part of his anatomy gave a peppy jerk. He warned himself to stop staring—to be practical— but as in his office this afternoon, he was incapable of either.

His eyes reached the short, white, belted coat with big black buttons and continued to dark blond hair framing her beautiful face. A staggeringly gorgeous face. A face he'd have sworn to his brother before last weekend was passably pretty.

A lie.

Taylor, with her slightly parted full lips, high cheekbones dusted pink and long black lashes shielding shimmering brown eyes wasn't "passably" anything.

She was an absolute knockout.

"Good evening." She said it as sweetly as Red Riding Hood, but the twitch in her smile was almost predatory. Before he could warn himself to be practical again, before he could rein in his hope that she'd come here for a reason that was as far away from professional as imaginable, his father's words revisited him like the Ghost of Longing Past.

"You're also careful in the wrong ways. Being reckless is okay from time to time."

No, the world hadn't flown off the axis when he'd kissed Taylor—in fact, things were going his way. Could be this was a sign that he was on the right track rather than the wrong one.

Lucky for her he was a safe Big Bad Wolf to her Red Riding Hood. With a grin he gestured to his foyer. "Won't you come in?"

Ten

Go big or go home.

That'd been Taylor's mantra through drying off after her shower and refreshing her one-and-a-half-inch-barrel curls. From smoothing body oil over her legs and arms to letting the La Perla slip and slide over her smooth, sensitive skin. She'd dug through her underwear drawer and found the matching lace thong. She hadn't worn the thong before either, having categorized it as something she'd wear "someday" like the lingerie.

But now that she was standing in Royce's foyer wearing nothing but silk and lace, now that her hands were nervously tightening the belt on her trench coat, she worried that she'd gone *too* big. That maybe she *should* go home.

"Perfect timing. I had no one to celebrate with and here you are. Can I interest you in a glass of wine?" Royce asked casually as if her showing up at his residence at 10:00 p.m. in do-me heels and a very short trench was normal behavior.

"Sure."

He took her clutch and keys from her shaking hands and gestured to the closet in the foyer. "You can hang your coat if you like."

She worried for a hot second that he had X-ray vision and knew exactly what she wore beneath her coat—that he'd gleaned the real reason she'd come here.

"No. Thank you. I'm, uh…cold."

He dipped his head in a short nod, his expression revealing none of his thoughts. "Red Zin should help with that."

He moved to the kitchen and she walked into the living room. She'd been here once, shortly after he'd moved in five or six years ago. It'd been a great space then but lacked the warmth it exuded now. The cigar-colored leather couch and modern gas fireplace in the center of the wall made her want to curl up in her jammies with a good book.

"Your wine." A balloon-shaped, stemless glass appeared in front of her and she took it, ignoring that her palms were starting to sweat.

Her previous roar of womanhood had turned into a kitten's mew.

How disappointing.

Worse, her confidence was flagging. It was possible she'd read Royce's reaction today wrong. Maybe he hadn't been checking her out. Maybe for him, peeking at her cleavage was no more interesting than…than… the plant in his foyer. Was that so unbelievable? That he *could* resist her?

Ugh.

"Royce, listen…" Setting the wineglass down, she faced him, ready to excuse herself and apologize for barging in. She wasn't prepared to confess the truth, but the excuse of work might be plausible enough to explain away her being here.

Maybe.

"Have you changed your mind about the coat?" His question startled her speechless. She'd never felt so vulnerable in her life.

If she said no, she could blather on about Lowell Olsen some more, saying how she wanted to discuss strategies. Royce would listen patiently, dole out advice and then she'd be on her way home no worse for wear.

But if she said yes… If she allowed Royce to peel her out of the coat and stood before him in her underwear, well… There'd be no explaining away why she was here, would there?

She was at the ultimate point of no return.

He might wrap her up in her coat—or hell, the nearest blanket—and command her to "go home, young lady." Okay, probably he wouldn't say that, but the sentiment would be implied. She was younger than him by six years, and hadn't his age been trotted out as one of the reasons she wasn't supposed to take an interest in him?

It was possible that, aside from the anomaly at the gala, he *still* saw her as his youngest sister's best friend. Not a woman who wanted to strip him out of his suit and spend a good deal of time with him naked.

Fear pressed against the base of her throat as she considered the likelihood that she'd blown his behavior this week out of proportion. Maybe his slow glances weren't interest, but mere curiosity.

"Taylor?" His eyebrows pinched in confusion. This was her chance to undo the potentially cataclysmic choice she'd made to come here. Possibly her last chance to escape unscathed.

But another deeply rooted desire shouted in protest. This was also her last chance to grab hold of what she wanted. She'd never had a rebellious streak. Why not start now?

Royce's hand hovered in midair, poised to take her coat if she was brave enough to hand it over.

"So?" the horned devil on her shoulder whispered, "What's it going to be?" Before Taylor could consult the angel on her other shoulder, the winged-and-haloed hussy nodded her encouragement.

Damned if she did… Damned if she didn't.

"Yes." When the word eked past her throat she couldn't believe she'd actually said it. And when she reached for his hand and placed it over the knot on her trench coat, it was like watching a scene in a movie. "I want you to take it off."

Hand resting over one of his, her heart thundering so loud she could scarcely hear her own erratic breathing, she watched as his other hand joined the first. As his fingers began to gently unknot the belt at her waist...

For once, the pragmatic side of Royce's mind was as silent as if it'd been bound and gagged. There was another side of him, an animalistic side whose instincts trumped reason, that was in charge now.

Knot undone, he opened Taylor's coat, his fingers twitching over what he'd found beneath. Black silk with a subtle shimmer glided over her barely dressed body. She shifted and the material slipped tantalizingly over her breasts, drawing his attention to their hardening peaks.

This was no dress. This was sex sewn together with lace.

He consulted her face for a beat and in her expression found approval—and a question. Did he like what he saw?

"This is a pleasant surprise," he murmured.

Relief washed over her. "I was hoping you'd say that."

"Was there another option?"

"You could tell me to put my coat on and go home."

He couldn't imagine a scenario in which he said that. He slowly removed her coat from her shoulders. "Is that what you want?"

Her head shook back and forth. *No.*

Good. That sure as hell wasn't what he wanted. Draping the coat over the back of the couch, he slid his fingers over the impossibly smooth material wanting to touch her bare skin beneath it, which he'd bet was equally smooth. She smelled good, like the bowl of lemons on his countertop—a light citrusy scent that reminded him of summer. She brought her own sunshine on this February night, her eyes bright and earnest, her body arching toward him as he pulled her closer. And when he set his mouth to hers, she responded in the best way imaginable.

She crashed into him lips first, her hands smoothing over his button-down shirt, moving from his pectorals to his shoulders and around to the back of his head, where she gripped his hair.

He sneaked his tongue into her mouth and encountered her equally eager tongue, and the rest of his body moved closer to her as well. Hips first, he ground his erection against her center. A sultry moan sounded in her throat.

He left the haven of her mouth to kiss the gentle curve of her throat before moving to the sensitive skin behind her ear. Hands smoothing over her ribs, he hesitated at the swells of her generous breasts, giving her a chance to push him away. To stop the forward motion that began with her showing up at his house in naught but a scrap of silk and the tallest shoes he'd ever seen her wear.

Instead of stopping him, she cupped his hand and laid it over one breast, tugging his mouth to hers and renewing her efforts to kiss him stupid. With the thumb of his right hand he brushed over her nipple, his left hand joining in so that her other breast wasn't neglected.

She hissed his name on a tight breath, her eyes shut and head dropping back.

"Is this what you came for tonight, Taylor?" Confidence made his voice a growl.

Rarely did he indulge in decadence, save a tall slice of chocolate cake now and then when a craving hit. Taylor wasn't unlike the sinful dessert, her layers exposed. He knew once he took that first taste, he'd devour all of her.

"Yes, but…"

"But?" He lifted his head to watch her.

"I wasn't sure if you'd respond…favorably."

Taking one of her hands, he pressed it against his crotch, straining forward so she could feel just how "favorably" he'd reacted. Her pupils widened, all but swallowing the soft green-brown irises.

"Are you sure this is what you want?" The beast he'd unleashed howled in protest, but he needed her to be sure before they went any further. He'd been swept up before and wouldn't go in blindly again.

"Are you?" She stuck a finger in the knot of his bow tie and tugged. The rasping sound as she slid it from his collar sent goose bumps down his arms. She tossed the tie onto the floor, one eyebrow arched in question. "You didn't seem interested earlier today."

"I was at work." And trying his damnedest to focus. "What did you expect me to do?"

"Fair point." She smoothed her hands over his

shoulders. He liked the way she looked at him, like he was a meal and she was starving.

His mind blanked of all thoughts save one: *Take her. Show her how beautiful and brave she is for showing up for you.*

Right when he needed her. Right where he wanted her. Before he'd known it himself.

He bent at the knees to smooth his palms under the lacy, satiny number and over her bare bottom. Thumb tracing the strap of her thong, it was his turn to groan.

He opened his mouth over her breast and lightly bit her nipple through the fabric. She clutched the back of his hair, her reaction an encouraging, "Oh God, Royce."

A wolfish grin emerged as he swept his mouth from her breast and slipped the thin straps off her shoulders. He bared her breasts and shimmied the material past her hips. It fell into a tiny black pool at her feet. One he could've sworn he'd fallen into, and was now careening into oblivion.

Tongue tracing her bare, puckered nipple, he slid one hand beneath the material of her thong, encountering her wetness. She tipped forward to ride his fingers, every slick, smooth glide sending his erection from rigid to damn painful. The torture was exquisite. He returned the favor, his mission to find out how much teasing she could stand. He suckled her nipple as she sighed his name.

"Yes, yes," came her next frantic whisper. She rode his hand in desperation, seeking her release. "Royce, please."

He straightened, his fingers moving double time against her, his eyes burning into hers. He wanted to watch her when she came. Watch her come apart in his hands, revel in the moment she achieved what she'd come here for: a powerful, and he'd bet beautiful, orgasm.

"What do you want, Taylor?" he asked with calm authority.

"This." Eyes closed, she held his shoulders for purchase.

"Describe 'this.'" He knew, but wanted to hear her say it. "Tell me. Please."

It was the *please* that tipped her. Her eyelids opened and her lust-blown gaze landed on his. "You. Touching me."

"Touching you how?" His control ebbed, his cock surging toward the woman who was making him want the one thing he shouldn't. *Her.*

Only now he couldn't remember why he shouldn't. Something about work and transition… Or was it that she was a colleague and they had to be a unified force…

The jumble of words in his head knotted themselves into a tangle. He couldn't focus on anything but the woman in his arms.

"I need… I need…" Her brows bent, her mouth dropping open as her cheeks flushed. He watched her face contort and felt the warm rush of moisture on his fingers. When her knees slackened, he locked an arm around her waist and held her up. She drooped her arms around his neck lazily.

Seconds later, she blew out a breath that ended on a soft, satisfied hum.

"You're gorgeous when you come, Taylor."

An ethereal goddess, to be precise.

Her smile spread on her face like honey dripping off warm toast, her front teeth stabbing her bottom lip as she fisted back his hair. "I bet you are, too."

He liked her boldness. She'd always possessed that attribute but until the gala it'd never been directed toward him. When she kissed him, it sent him into a weightless, uncontrolled spin. He couldn't seem to find "up" again, couldn't make himself care about the consequences he'd held so precious not long ago.

"Only one way to find out," he heard himself say.

Lifting her naked body into his arms, he carried her to the couch. The moment her back hit the leather she began working his belt through the buckle.

Eleven

She'd had no idea what to name the craving that had shaken her for the last week, but now she understood what the hunger had been about. What she'd been hungry for was *him*.

Before Royce sent his fingers into a one-man banjo solo over the most sensitive part of her body, she'd have sworn she was doing fine on her own in that department. What could possibly be the difference between a man's fingers and her own?

Now she had no idea where to start counting. The rough pads versus smooth? The not knowing what he would do next versus her own evenly timed strokes? Or the dirty, delicious way he talked to her during?

Yes. To all of the above.

Aftershocks shook her shoulders as she relived the best orgasm she'd had in literally *years*.

But she couldn't chastise herself for not sleeping with someone sooner. Instinctually she knew that anyone other than Royce wouldn't have delivered as well.

Even after he removed her coat she'd half expected him to turn her down. With him, calm practicality reigned supreme.

Not this version of him, though. He was different tonight. Looser and more open. Eager to please her.

Royce pushed his slacks along with his boxer briefs off his muscular legs. He stood before her, his heavy erection standing against a backdrop of ab muscles she'd had no idea were there. His lips twitched into a smile as he peeled the starched white shirt from his glorious chest. The right amount of wiry hair dusted his pecs and led from his belly button to the part of him she couldn't wait to experience.

The dampness between her legs renewed, a warm trickle sliding through her as she mentally prepared for all that length, all that strength covering her. Clothes in hand, he tucked them against his body and bent to kiss her lightly on the mouth. "Be back."

"Wh-where are you going?" She propped herself up on her elbows, watching his clenching and contracting ass moved away from her and down the hallway.

"Condom," he called as he vanished into the darkness.

Right. Protection. She eased down on the couch,

allowing herself a small laugh at her forgetfulness— or maybe it was the sheer joy of getting exactly what she wanted with relative ease.

He didn't stay gone long, padding barefoot back to her. His hand wrapped around himself, he rolled on the protection she was glad one of them remembered. He lowered himself onto the couch and she parted her thighs to accept him. His warm-bordering-hot skin came in contact with her greedy nipples and she gasped at the sensation.

"I like your hair this way." He wrapped one of her curls around his finger. "I noticed it this morning."

"That wasn't all you noticed."

Looking over his shoulder at the high heels still strapped to her feet, he gave her a feral grin. "Lock those around my thighs."

She did as she was told, her body naturally tilting to accept him. When he nudged her entrance she accepted him inch by glorious inch, but made sure she kept her eyes open. Watching him endure the slow torture of entering her was sheer joy, and one he savored. He stretched her intentionally before he began to move. Seated to the root, he let out a sound resembling a growl.

"You looked as innocent as Red Riding Hood on my porch, but there was something wild in your eyes."

"Wild, as in unhinged?" A breath hissed from between her teeth as he pulled out and slid in again—so smooth, so good.

"Wild, as in you're not as safe as you look."

"Are you the wolf in this scenario?" She toyed

with his hair, loving talking during sex. Unique, this entire encounter.

"Maybe we're both wolves." His next thrust wasn't as careful as the one before it, brushing her G-spot and causing her brain to skip like a smooth rock over a still pond.

Before she sank beneath the surface she forced him back into focus. "You're the wolf."

He winked. Winked!

"I like you like this," she said, unsure what she'd meant by that until she continued speaking. "Unable to resist me."

"You make it hard, Taylor Thompson."

"Quite the double entendre."

"Keep up that smart mouth and I'll double my efforts."

"Threat or promise?"

He was still for a second. "A threat you'll beg for after how good I make you feel." He kissed her lips quickly.

Proving his ability to blot out her mind, he doubled his efforts. Each stroke deeper, more frantic. Her fingernails dragged down the skin of his back, leaving stripes. She fought to hold on to him while slipping off the side of the planet. Voice strained with effort, he said, "Let's see that O face again, Red."

"Let's see if you can bring it, *Wolf*." It was a challenge he accepted.

He nestled one of her knees in the crook of his elbow, lifting her leg and deepening their connection. She couldn't form any words other than "Yes, Royce, yes."

Pleased by her reaction, his smile turned rogue. Refusing to go into the abyss alone, she gripped him with her internal muscles. Surprise colored his face for a beat before he captured her mouth with his.

Seconds later, his head bucked. He bared his teeth, his hips pistoning, the slick skin of their thighs gently slapping. She watched the entire display, smugly satisfied to have her theory proven.

He was *quite* gorgeous when coming.

"They're clean." Royce handed over a pair of leggings and an MIT sweatshirt. "Gia stopped by here to change for the gala and left them. They've been laundered."

He announced it evenly, as if having his clothes laundered rather than doing it himself was a normal, everyday occurrence. She supposed for the Knox family it was. She'd never seen Gia load a washing machine.

When Taylor moved from her parents' house and rented her sizable apartment, she found she enjoyed cleaning her own space. As soon as she was promoted to COO and her hours increased, she hired a part-time housekeeper. With the hours she worked, it was impossible to do it all, but she kept a few tasks on her own to-do list.

One, cooking—the kitchen was a bright, open space that sparked her creativity—and two, her laundry. It wasn't about finding joy in domesticity, a trait she definitely *hadn't* inherited from her mother. She was particular about her clothes and what didn't have to be dry-cleaned she cared for herself. It didn't make sense for Royce, with his array of starched shirts and suits and bow ties, to stand around doing the wash.

"Thanks." She accepted the clothes, covering herself with the slip first. She was strangely nervous now that they'd had sex, and him standing over her made her feel more vulnerable. "Could you...?"

"Oh. Sorry. I'll give you a minute." His frown returned like it'd never left and she wondered if she'd imagined the smooth-talking, smiling man who'd just turned her inside out.

Neither of them reacted as expected. She'd come here to seduce him, until her spine had turned temporarily weak. He'd reacted the complete opposite—pouncing on her the second she gave the okay.

"No. Wait. Sit down." She lifted her hips and rolled on her thong as discreetly as possible. Royce sat, his eyes glued to her legs. "We don't have to make this weird."

"Too late." His dry tone held a note of humor.

She tugged on the black leggings next, grateful to Gia for leaving them behind. As the clock ticked on, the temperature was dropping. Taylor didn't want to drive home wearing only a slip and a tiny trench coat if she didn't have to.

"No, we don't have to make this weird." He leaned an elbow on the arm of the sofa and raised his wineglass as she pulled the sweatshirt over her head. It was butter-soft and elephant gray, the wide neck falling off one of her shoulders. Royce's eyes didn't leave that swatch of bared skin, where the strap of her slip was visible.

"So." She lifted her wineglass, too, snuggling into the opposite corner of his couch. "It's taken ten years for you to notice I'm a woman."

He rolled the wine around his mouth before swallowing. "I noticed."

"You did?" That shocked her down to her chilly toes.

He chuckled, his chest expanding within the deep navy blue T-shirt he'd paired with baggy pajama bottoms. His feet were bare. He had nice feet. Big feet, but nice. She'd never dated a guy who wore pajama bottoms, had she? Sweats, yes; boxers, sure; but cotton pajama bottoms with skinny navy blue pinstripes? Not that she could recall.

"I'm surprised you care," he said.

She made a choking sound in the back of her throat.

"Not a blow-off," he amended. "More an honest observation. You were Gia's best friend, closer to Brannon's age than mine. What would an eighteen-year-old want from a twenty-four-year-old, anyway? Did you expect me to scoop you up and steal away your virginity?"

"Joke would've been on you since I'd lost my virginity two years prior." She hoisted an eyebrow, pleased when his lips twitched. "You were twenty-four, not forty-four. It wouldn't have been that unbelievable for us to date back then." But even as she said it, she had her doubts. He'd had his sights set on college girls, not a high school senior who dreaded showing up to every richie-rich function their parents made them attend. He'd had no clue she'd watched him, admiring his breadth and height. The way he held himself. Always the confident one, his walk tall and words evenly spaced. Bran was quicker to laugh and less serious, which she enjoyed in a friendship, but boyfriend material to her was and always would be a man she could count on.

Like my father.

She swallowed the unexpected lump of emotion and swiftly changed the subject. "You could have asked me to be your date at any one of the charity functions I had to be dragged to."

"And here we are a decade later still attending them." His tone hinted that he found them as asinine as she did.

"You don't enjoy going?" She genuinely believed Royce didn't mind attending stuffy functions and donning tuxedos and bow ties. He fit in, drink in hand, genial expression on his face no matter who he was conversing with.

"Hide it well, don't I?" He lifted an eyebrow. The slightly roguish expression went well with his relaxed attire and the sex-warmed buzz vibrating her limbs.

"You hide lots of things well." The words were muttered against the rim of her wine glass. She liked sharing this slice of time with him. In his space, the fire burning in front of them—the one burning *between* them. She liked sharing wine and truths while sitting three feet apart.

"I do what's expected of me. Always have." He shrugged. "Consummate firstborn."

She was sure the last thing anyone would "expect" was for him to take Taylor Thompson to bed—er, to couch. And no one would have put money on her showing up to seduce him, either. A bubble of pride lifted her chest. Finally, she'd taken what she wanted.

"The Valentine's Day gala has always been my least favorite. Until this year. *Coincidentally.*"

She caught his heated gaze and returned it, the air between them practically igniting. He cupped her toes with one large, warm hand.

"Want some socks too?"

"Thanks, but I have to strap those puppies back on." She pointed to the shoes beneath the coffee table, which were about as inviting as an iron maiden. She'd kicked them off when he went to change, past ready to give her toes a break.

"I like them, if it's any consolation." He gave her foot a squeeze, a gesture that felt familiar even though it'd never happened before.

"I bet I was the last person you expected to find standing on your porch tonight." It'd been outrageous to expect sex simply because she showed up almost naked, but her instincts were rarely wrong.

"The very last. I half thought you were Bran coming to kick my ass. Figured Dad told him…" His lips pressed together like he'd said too much. "Never-mind."

Did he really expect her to let a whopper like that one go?

"What? What did you think Jack told him?"

Tongue swiping his bottom lip, Royce seemed to turn over telling her versus not. He stood and crossed the room to fetch a thin blanket, tossing it over her before he continued, which was sweet.

Wineglass in hand, he watched out the large window behind the dining room table.

"CEO is mine."

She blinked, shocked. She couldn't have been more surprised if she'd found Royce standing at *her* front door wearing naught but a trench coat.

"How…do you feel about it?" She had to ask. She couldn't read his tone or his body language.

"It's my responsibility."

"Do you want it?"

"Of course," he snapped. A warning. Best not to push the topic. They slept together but it didn't grant her entry into his inner circle.

Boundaries were important. They had a lot at stake—more now that Royce was going to be named CEO. Sneaking around wasn't the wisest course of action.

"I should go." She threw off the blanket. "Early day tomorrow. Breakfast with my mom."

He didn't argue, but what had she expected? A heartfelt plea that she strip out of her clothes and follow him to the bedroom? Romance wasn't in the cards for them—especially when she'd started them

off on a very unromantic note. Sexy yes, romantic…
Not so much.

She buckled her uncomfortable shoes and stood.
Royce followed behind her without a second's hes-
itation. Once they entered the mouth of the foyer,
he handed over her clutch and keys. Outside a crisp
breeze blew the palm fronds overhead, black against
a blacker night sky.

"Good night." Sweeping her hair behind her ears,
she guessed a good-night kiss was pushing it. "Congratulations. On CEO."

She turned to walk to her car parked in the driveway when he said her name. Hope rose fierce and
full, pressing against her breastbone.

Ask me to stay.

He descended one porch step, all that capable mas-
culine beauty hovering over her. Then he opened his
mouth and "Don't say anything to Brannon or Gia"
came out.

"Oh. Sure." She nodded. That hope deflated, going
limp in her chest and sagging her lungs.

He folded his arms over his chest to ward off the
air's chill. "Mom and Dad want to tell them sepa-
rately. Before the official announcement is made at
the ThomKnox offices."

Words failed her.

He nodded, a succinct dip of his chin before he
walked back inside and shut the door.

So much for romance.

Twelve

Jack Knox's birthday dinner was held at the Hour-glass, a posh fourteen-room hotel in San Francisco that was formerly, of all things, a marble factory. Recently overhauled and designed by Mercury Hill, an acclaimed architecture firm, the building echoed elegance from a hundred years ago while still maintaining a bohemian feel.

The backdrop of the bar was chalkboard-black wood, the floors were a herringbone pattern, and the columns black with contrasting white wood grain. Curved, stuffed chairs in tones of brick red, olive green and deep gray surrounded brass-edged tables dotted with cocktail napkins, on which sat a variety of glasses. Lowball, highball, flutes and the occasional beer glass.

Royce arrived by car, Gia in tow. It occurred to him to invite Taylor to join them, but since he wouldn't have normally asked her to join him, he didn't. The way they'd parted last night left him confused, but then he wasn't great at reading women—this woman in particular.

He preferred his situations black-and-white, like a spreadsheet. Each bit of information in a clearly marked box. Outlined. Precise. Relationships, and women in general, were not so easily contained.

Taylor was about as navigable as a ship in a storm.

They'd had sex—exquisite sex. Did that mean he should call her? Were they dating? The more he thought about it, the more aggravated he became. He'd decided before he arrived to compartmentalize that bit of info. Tonight was about his father's birthday. That was it.

"The man of the hour is on his way!" Bran announced to the crowd, loud enough to be heard by those who had wandered out to the rooftop seating area. He pocketed his cell phone, his smile bright and his shoulders back. It was good to see him not pissed off. Royce guessed their parents hadn't broken the CEO news to him, or else his brother would be a lot less happy. He'd also noticed, during the hour-long drive with his sister, that Gia wasn't in the know, either. She undoubtedly would have brought it up.

"Scotch for you, sir." The bartender served Royce his drink.

"Thank you." Royce had been here for less than five minutes so he hadn't taken inventory of the room.

He guesstimated sixty-plus people in attendance for the party that was scheduled to start at eight o'clock, the man of the hour to arrive not fashionably late, but *Jack* late. Jack was on time when he needed to be— he never missed a meeting. But for casual functions like this one he kept his arrival to a fifteen-to-twenty-minute window after the party was scheduled to start. Royce would venture that everyone knew tonight had a twofold purpose for his father: a birthday celebration and a retirement announcement.

Taylor approached him wearing a basic black dress and a smile. Though modest, the frock sent his mind to the gutter. The skirt was knee length and hugged curves he now knew a lot about, and the neckline reminded him of her lingerie—her in it and out of it. Of her undulating beneath him, her mouth open to sigh his name. Of the thong he'd peeled off her long legs. He wondered if she wore a similar undergarment tonight. Judging by the soft outline of her breasts and shy press of her nipples against the fabric, she hadn't worn much beneath the dress.

"Hi," he said. Because *Are you wearing underwear?* wasn't polite.

"You made it." She carried an empty wineglass, apparently catching him on her return to the bar.

"White or red?" He took her glass.

"Rosé."

Leave it to Taylor to choose the undefinable in-between. He found himself smiling as he placed her order.

"Fitting," he said, handing her a full glass of pink

wine. But he meant more than her being in the middle of two certainties. "Nearly the color of your cheeks when you came to visit me last night."

Those murmured words took him by surprise—flirting wasn't exactly his MO—but Taylor always drew the unexpected from him.

She lifted her glass to her lips and the heavy gem-studded bangle on her wrist caught the overhead light.

"I've never been here before." She glanced around the room, the brass light fixtures bent to highlight the paintings on the wall, some of them fox-and-hound hunting paintings, others splashy abstracts that complemented the furniture.

"The bar is one of my favorites, and not only because they carry 1926 Macallan." He raised his own glass. "I like the chairs. They look like they belong in a seedy bar, but they're the finest leather, and damn comfortable."

"They snub pretension here."

"There's a painting of dogs playing poker in the men's lavatory."

Her eyes widened. "Really?"

"No." He grinned, enjoying teasing her.

She laughed, demurely tilting her head to the side. The move sent her hair over her shoulder, the blond and brown strands sliding into a unique pattern.

"You changed your hair."

"I had it done today." She sifted a hand through the silken locks and again he was drawn in by the way the various colors fell. "How observant of you."

He opened his mouth to tell her what he'd noticed

last night. The pink in her cheeks, the citrusy scent that clung to his skin after she left. The way her hair had tickled his arms whenever he drove into her. The way he woke up this morning with a hard-on, the echoes of her hoarse cries of completion ringing in his ears...

"Hello, good people." Bran swaggered over, beer in hand.

"Bran," Royce greeted.

Taylor put distance between herself and Royce, but Bran didn't seem to notice, leaning in to kiss her cheek.

"You look nice." She nodded approvingly at Bran's casual slacks and button-down.

Royce felt the uncomfortable prickle of jealousy. She hadn't mentioned his suit and bow tie ensemble.

"Ready for anything," Bran said, his gaze seeking the door again for their father's arrival.

Dammit. He doesn't know.

Jack was spontaneous. Liked the spotlight. Even though his father had told Royce he'd announce CEO in a meeting at work, part of him wondered if their father had something a bit more spontaneous in mind.

"There he is!" someone shouted, moving in from the rooftop toward the front door. Jack entered, their mother Macy on his arm, and lifted a hand to wave.

"Let the party begin!" Jack shouted when someone placed a drink in his hand.

Bran was the first to approach their father and embrace him, Gia second. Royce hung back, allowing close friends and coworkers to go ahead of him.

"Your dad. So *caj*," Taylor said next to his ear.

"What is that?"

"*Caj?* It's short for casual."

"Short for casual? Is it such a long word that we needed to shorten it?"

"Showing your age again, Royce." She winked, standing closer to allow space for the press of bodies that had gravitated toward Jack like he was sun to their planets.

"Which reminds me. I have to be in the car on my way home by nine."

"Oh?" He loved the look of disappointment that swam over her features. Like she'd miss him when he left.

"That's when I watch my true crime shows and work my evening crossword puzzle."

It took her a second to realize he was kidding. "Tease."

He leaned in, mostly to smell her lemony skin. "You started it."

She held his gaze, not bothering to move away from him this time. He liked being close to her. Without anyone in the way. Without any expectations. How rare for him to enjoy anything without expectations.

"Have you seen the rooftop?" he asked.

"But the guest of honor is in here." She pointed at Jack.

"No," Royce disagreed, taking her elbow. "She's right here."

He led them away from the crowd and onto the now-abandoned private rooftop.

Thirteen

The deep navy sky made up her third-favorite part of the ambience on the rooftop lounge. Closing in on second was the modern, square fire table surrounded by chairs. First place belonged to the man who'd walked her out here.

Royce's deep gray jacket was paired with dark trousers, and she caught a peek of suspenders over a crisp, white shirt when he'd turned to lead her outside. The bow tie was her favorite, though. Navy with a silver sheen, yet somehow casual enough to work with the rest of his outfit.

He undid a button on his jacket and pulled out a chair for her. She sat, curling her wine against her chest. Fire or not, the wind hit her and she bristled. A detail he noticed. A moment later her shoulders were covered by his suit jacket. He sat in the chair next to hers and she admired him unabashedly.

Suspenders. White shirt. Bow tie.

Purr.

She was so into him. After the awkward way they'd parted last night she hadn't expected him to be so open.

Jack Knox's laugh drew her attention. Inside, he tossed his white head back, his smile gleaming.

"He doesn't act sixty-something. But you do." She tilted her head at Royce. "Odd."

"Very funny." He canted an eyebrow.

"I didn't tell Gia or Bran, by the way. About us *or the other thing.*" She widened her eyes meaningfully.

"I figured. I rode here with her tonight. If Gia knew, she'd have brought it up. She's not one to keep her feelings to herself."

"I didn't realize you two came together."

He seemed to debate sharing more before saying, "Since her and Jayson's divorce, she leans on me as a travel companion. Don't tell her I told you that. She'll castrate me."

Taylor nodded. Her friend was independent, capable. Gia wouldn't want anyone to know she relied on her big brother for transportation.

"She did ask if there were any further developments where we were concerned." Royce sipped his drink, letting Taylor sweat that out for a few seconds before he shook his head. "I said no."

She didn't enjoy keeping secrets from her best friend, but until Taylor had a handle on what was going on with Royce, she wasn't going to tell Gia anything.

As if on cue, Gia's voice rose behind them. "So this is where the party's at!" She plopped down next to Royce and slapped his knee. "What up, bro?"

"We didn't want to interfere with the ass-kissing. How'd it go?" He swiped her nose with one finger and she glared.

"Don't give me that brownnose spiel. You're the one vying for CEO."

Royce's expression darkened as he exchanged glances with Taylor.

"They should put you in a ring and make you and Bran fight to the death. Like gladiators," Gia added gleefully. "Tay and I would enjoy that."

"There'll be no fighting to the death. Sorry to disappoint you. I will accept Dad's decision."

Gia grew silent, her gaze fastened to her oldest brother.

"What?" Royce's face was a neutral mask, but Gia reacted as if the truth were written on his forehead.

"It's you, isn't it?"

"I— How—"

Brannon's telltale good-natured laugh drifted over their heads next. He walked out, Cooper at his side, and joined their group. Gia kept an eye on Royce, but didn't say more.

An hour later, most of the sixty-eight guests— Addison counted—had left the party for a variety of reasons. The dozen or so of them remaining converged on the rooftop. Additional heaters on stands had been lit to thwart the cold, the flames reflecting off the six-foot-high glass overlooking the city. Above that barrier, a crescent moon stamped the center of a star-pocked sky.

Taylor was still wearing Royce's jacket, which was warm and smelled like him: *incredible*. No one had mentioned it, but Gia had given her a lengthy look that said *we'll talk later*.

Jayson Cooper sat next to Gia, a few inches between the two exes on a short white bench. Bran relaxed in a chair next to Taylor. They were talking about how ill-suited for retirement Jack was, and how gracefully he'd aged.

"I'm glad I inherited the thickness of his hair," Gia said. "But the headful of white can wait."

"What's this?" Cooper touched a strand of Gia's dark brown hair. "Looks like you're getting a head start."

"Stop it!" Gia slapped his hand away.

He grinned, and Taylor shook her head at Gia. "He's teasing you. Your hair is gray-free and beautiful. And still chestnut in color."

Cooper chuckled. "That gets her every time."

"This is why we're divorced." Gia's smile was patronizing.

"That and your inability to admit when I'm right," Coop replied with an easy smile.

Those two. Taylor shook her head, unsure what to make of their bickering. Sometimes it sounded like flirting, other times like they were navigating the difficult landscape of friendship after a divorce.

"I'd like to make a toast." Jack stepped out of the circle of people with whom he was conversing and raised his bottle of water. "And an announcement."

Royce once again looked to Taylor, and she schooled her expression. Only Jack knew what Jack planned on announcing, but judging by Royce's grim expression, she wondered if the CEO announcement would happen sooner than expected.

Jack Knox gestured to the glass wall surrounding the rooftop. "You know… I should've arranged for a group BASE jump while we're all here."

Royce shook his head, unsure if his old man was joking or not. Lately Jack had shown interest in a lot of adventurous pastimes, though diving off a building in a city was illegal, so hopefully he wasn't serious about that one.

"If you're here it's because I've asked you not to leave." Jack switched gears with a jolt. "Not to worry, the staff was polite when they used cattle prods to blast those others out of here early."

In the remaining crowd were Royce's parents, his siblings, Taylor, Taylor's mother, Deena, who'd arrived about an hour ago, Addison, Whitney and a handful of others from the board and upper management. All trusted insiders.

"Thank you for making my sixty-second birthday special." Jack walked through the crowd while he talked. "I never thought ThomKnox would grow to be as big as it is. When Charlie and I started this company we wanted to avoid the confines of a big corporate office while giving ourselves—and the people who work for us—the trappings of a great place life. Then, my children joined the ranks." He cupped Bran's shoulder before resting a hand on Taylor's shoulder next. "And Charlie's daughter."

Her smile was pained yet grateful, with another emotion behind it Royce couldn't place. It uncoiled a sense of longing within him he didn't recognize. He *wanted* to know what emotions had splintered her smile. And why.

Another new reaction to this woman. They just kept coming.

"I didn't expect to be a tech leader, but what I really didn't expect was for Charles to be gone." Jack squeezed Taylor's shoulder and her eyes closed.

Losing Charles was still fresh. Grief rang tuning-fork true when Jack moved to Deena and softly kissed her cheek.

"We've reached yet another fork in the road of ThomKnox," Jack said. "I'm not getting any younger, and if you ask Macy she'll tell you I'm trying my damnedest to age backward."

"It's true," his mother addressed the crowd. "Just ask our new Ferrari."

The crowd laughed on cue.

Jack held out a hand to quiet them. "It's time for me to go and do some of those things Charlie and I imagined we'd do after retirement. But I am leaving you in capable hands in my absence. Brannon has served as President and our darling genius daughter, who inherited her father's legendary brains, has kept us on the edge of relevance, along with our own tech superhero Jayson Cooper."

"How smart can she be if she let me go?" Cooper draped his arm over his ex-wife's shoulders and pulled her close to kiss her temple.

"You're a moron," Gia told him, but she smiled anyway.

"And Royce." Standing behind him now, Jack cupped his oldest son's shoulder. "Royce has been CFO for as long as I can remember. He's the nerdiest of all of us, and that's saying something for a tech company." More laughter.

Royce's grimace wasn't due to his father's jibes, but at the premonition of where this speech would end.

"He's capable," Jack continued, "he's confident. And as of now, he's your new CEO."

The announcement was made in the same easygoing tone as the rest of the speech. A palpable silence fell as the crowd absorbed the news.

Jack Knox had named his successor.

"I knew it!" Gia was the first to say.

Bran frowned.

"To Royce!" Jack raised his water bottle and a smattering of "cheers" and "congratulations" lifted one after another in clunky refrain.

"Speech!" someone called. "Speech! Speech!"

Dammit, Dad.

This wasn't how the announcement should've happened. There was *supposed* to be a discussion ahead of time with Bran and Gia. They were *supposed* to be in a meeting at work with a bullet-pointed agenda. Jack wanted a BASE jump? This bombshell came close.

"Go on, son. Address your underlings," Jack said.

Royce stood, his glare affixed on his father. "We had an agreement."

Jack shrugged with his mouth. "Things change."

Royce took a long look at the man he'd admired his entire life and realized he was too angry to say anything productive. So instead he turned to Cooper and asked, "Can you give Gia a ride home?"

"Um…" Jayson looked at Gia.

"I'll give Gia a ride home," Taylor offered with a subtle nod. One that said *Go. I have this.*

So he turned on his heel and left.

Without giving a damn speech.

"Two rosés, please," Gia told the bartender at her apartment's lobby bar.

"I can't," Taylor told her. "I'll sit with you, though." The glass and a half of rosé at the party felt like it was still sitting in her throat after Royce's surprising exit.

"No speech then," Jack had said to the crowd, but the comment didn't earn many smiles. Tension was thick in the air. The music started up again and, little by little, conversations restarted. Bran had been silent, his face unreadable. Gia's wasn't as much of a mystery.

They'd stayed only fifteen minutes or so more before Gia hooked Taylor's arm and suggested they leave, too. Fine by Taylor. She'd had enough of the strange evening.

Now, wineglasses in front of them, Gia pushed Taylor's closer. "Just one."

She couldn't turn down her friend. They needed to talk anyway and what Taylor had to say was best discussed over even the most meager amount of alcohol.

"No gray hairs, you swear?"

Taylor held up a palm. "Hand to God."

"Jay." Gia shook her head. "When is he going to back off and get a life?"

"When are you?" Taylor teased, raising an eyebrow.

"Bitch!" Gia laughed the word, giving Taylor a playful shove in the arm before laying her head on Taylor's shoulder. "You'd think he'd have found some new woman to tease."

"You'll always be teased by Jayson Cooper," Taylor said, confident she was right. "Has he even been on a date since you two split?"

"God. I hope so. I hope both of us haven't been celibate for the last year-plus."

"You'd have my sympathy if I hadn't gone *two* years before sleeping with someone." Taylor sipped her wine, not realizing until her friend's mouth dropped open that she'd just confessed the end to her own celibacy.

"*Who?* Who did you sleep with recently?" Gia had been Taylor's own personal cheerleader these last few years. Taylor had confessed she didn't feel anything sexually after Seth left. Her father's diagnosis had only added to her brokenness. Gia had comforted her, saying, "When you're ready, you'll know. No rush."

Taylor took a gulp of her wine, though fortifying herself with the drink meant sticking around longer than she intended. "Before I tell you, you have to promise not to be mad."

"Oh shit. You slept with Brannon?"

"No. I slept with Royce."

Gia's dark eyes rounded. She hadn't been expecting that. "Royce as in my oldest, glorified accountant brother?"

"That's the one. I showed up at his house last night wearing that La Perla slip I've had for way too long."

Gia gaped at her. "Why?"

Valid question.

"My dad."

Her friend's eyebrows rose.

"He cautioned me against dating Royce over the years. Said he was too old for me. I guess after the kiss at the gala, and the way Royce has been looking at me…"

"He's been *looking* at you? Why didn't you tell me any of this!" Gia's tone was accusatory, and deservedly so. Taylor normally told her friend everything.

"I wasn't sure. He's run a little hot and cold. Until last night. Then it was full-blast *hot*."

"Man." Gia shook her head. "How did I miss that tonight?"

"We're good actors."

"Well, how was it?"

"How was what?" Taylor spun her glass on the bar top and feigned ignorance.

"The sex," Gia said. Loudly. The bartender blinked from his computer screen over to them until Gia addressed him with a stern, "Do you mind?"

"Let's say it was a hell of a way to end the drought," Taylor said meaningfully.

"Wow. I have been in the dark."

"It only happened last night."

"Did you know about CEO, too?" Gia had easily fit those two puzzle pieces together.

"I did. But in Royce's defense, your dad asked him not to say anything to you or Bran. Jack was supposed to tell you and then announce it in a meeting."

"Leave it to Dad to make a scene." Gia chewed on her lip. "I couldn't tell if Bran was okay or not."

When they left, Bran was talking with Addison, and the conversation appeared intense. Taylor wondered if Bran had been using Addi as a distraction to avoid talking to his father.

"Well. Brannon is a grown man," Gia said in conclusion. "And you two are okay, right?"

"Yes, completely. I think you were close when you guessed he was proposing to win CEO. He'd die before he'd admit that was true."

"I'll strangle him after I strangle Royce for not telling me about CEO." Gia sighed. "Did you eat enough at the party?"

"Not even close."

"No one can survive on canapés alone." Gia waved over the bartender. "What's your best appetizer?"

"I'm trained to say they're all good, but for my money you can't beat the spinach dip or the fried pepper jack cheese bites."

"Both?" Gia asked Taylor.

"Both," she confirmed.

Fourteen

After the new CEO was announced on Monday morning, the offices at ThomKnox were buzzing with excitement—and gossip. Taylor had plenty to handle without the nervous phone calls, emails and sideline chats from the legion of managers she oversaw. The captain of the ship was retiring and with that guard change came a lot of nervousness and fear.

Will this change my retirement plans?

Are there other changes to management?

Will my department be restructured?

And so on and so on.

On Tuesday morning, when she'd dared poke her head out of her own office, she'd witnessed a heated conversation going on in Royce's office. Brannon, Jack and Royce were all in there, and while she couldn't hear their voices, the expressions on their faces through the window suggested they weren't exactly *simpatico*.

The week that was long by Tuesday felt like it'd lasted a month by Friday's tablet commercial premiere. The executive conference room was packed with upper-crust ThomKnox management, Jack included.

"This will be my last meeting," he announced. "But I couldn't miss sharing the commercial for our new tablet, the T13. This seven-minute commercial was directed and designed by Downey Design out of Chicago..."

While Jack spoke, Taylor took the temperature of the room. Gia tapped a rose gold pen on her planner, listening—or acting like she was listening. Cooper was leaned back in a chair, arms folded, also listening. Brannon was glaring at Royce and Royce glaring back at him.

So.

There were some unresolved issues.

"Let's have a look, shall we?" Jack shut off the lights and played the commercial.

The video was dark, a ribbon of light sweeping along the edge of a streamlined tablet that looked more like a curvy sports car than a flat computer.

Royce leaned back in his chair and whatever pheromones had been dormant this week permeated the air around her. The room was dark, her senses heightened. She felt him shift infinitesimally closer, and when she heard his rough exhale she recalled the way his warm breath coasted along her neck the last time he kissed her. When he cleared his throat she heard his phantom commands. *Come for me, Taylor. Now.*

Fantasies had plagued her even though she'd been away from him for a week. She considered how right he was about suggesting they keep their distance during such a monumental power shift at work. This was a distraction none of them needed.

It'd been easy to avoid him during the hectic week, but now that they were in this dark room, side by side—

One of Royce's fingers skimmed over her hand and then along her wrist. She sucked in a sharp breath. He tickled her wrist along the edge of her bracelet and she swallowed down a lump of lust. Innocuous, that touch. A mere brush of his skin on hers. And yet she shifted in her seat, distracted and turned on.

She checked to see if anyone noticed. Everyone watched the screen while the voice-over described the stunning new features of the T13. She should be watching, too, but she couldn't concentrate on anything save Royce's hand, now stroking her leg.

He brushed her knee, then higher. The rhythm he set—slow, firm, a whisper of a touch and then a gentle squeeze—was driving her wild. She leaned forward and pretended to write on the notebook in front of her.

The video reached its crescendo as his warm hand slipped beneath her skirt and he gripped her inner thigh firmly. She wouldn't dare look at him. Wouldn't show him the desire in her eyes, igniting her every limb.

Evidently he didn't need the encouragement. He

tickled her knee one last time before pulling his hand away. In the dim light, he raised his eyebrows as if to say *Your turn*.

He was challenging her?

Not wise, Knox.

After a furtive glance around the room, she slid her palm over his thigh and higher. He jerked in his seat, feigning a cough while he shifted in his chair. Her Cheshire smile would've been obvious if anyone was looking at her, but they weren't. She palmed Royce's crotch and met his dark gaze in the darker room. His intense expression was highlighted by the glow of the screen. They locked eyes for a beat, then two, before she swept her hand from his hardening cock.

She exhaled slowly, her heart racing, her body warm and ready. Where was a closet when you needed one? She wanted nothing more than to grab him by the ears and kiss him until both of them were gasping for breath or tearing at each other's clothes. Whichever came first.

Applause jolted her out of her stupor, and the lights slowly rose. Royce looked equally shell-shocked, though a better word might be *horny*.

"Thoughts?" Jack asked the room before taking his chair next to Royce. "Let's start with you, CEO."

Royce, scrumptiously flustered, straightened his bow tie. "I'm intrigued. At first I thought it wasn't for me. A version of this product has been around for years and I've never once been tempted. But this tease—" He gestured to the screen, but Taylor knew exactly what—*who*—he was talking about. "I've changed my mind. It's too sexy to ignore. It's unforgettable. I want more." He slanted a heated look at her. "What about you, COO?"

She ignored the warmth of her cheeks and addressed him directly. "I've had my eye on this one for a while. I was waiting for the right moment to bring it into my life. It could be the game changer I didn't know I was looking for."

The comments continued around the room. Her eyes watched her coworkers but her body was focused on only one person. The man she couldn't keep her head or hands off—the man she didn't want to keep her hands off any longer… Damn the consequences.

The executive team filed out of the conference room, Royce in the lead. He paused to open the door for Taylor, who put extra wiggle in her walk for his benefit. His eyes were glued to her ass, tucked neatly into a navy blue dress. Her tall red high heels were distracting to the nth degree.

Royce waited at the door watching everyone leave. Brannon hung back, as did Jack.

Gia turned to Royce, her attitude set to stun. "Are you guys over your snit?"

Thinking she was referring to him and Taylor, he wisely didn't speak.

"Subtle, Gia," Brannon said. "What'd you expect me to do? Overturn the conference table?"

Ah. She was referring to the heated discussion between Jack, Bran and Royce earlier this week in Royce's office.

"We have a company to run, boys," she said to her brothers. To Dad, she said, "Except for you. Aren't you retired?"

"Yes, and none of this is my problem." He gestured to his sons before leaving the room. "These two need to box it out."

Royce grunted. He and Brannon had argued over the years but it'd never resulted in a physical altercation.

"If you'll excuse me. Presidential duties await." Bran shouldered past them and stalked toward his office, his walk tall and his shoulders back.

They'd be okay. Probably.

The complaint wasn't that Royce had inherited CEO but that he'd kept learning of it a secret. Instead of blaming Dad for the subterfuge, his siblings were content to pin it on Royce. Blame must've come with the new title.

"And you." Gia stabbed Royce with one finger. "Taylor? Were you going to tell me?"

He made sure no one was eavesdropping before responding, his voice low. "No. I don't normally consult you about the women in my bed."

Taylor had told Gia after all. But they were close. It was bound to come out.

"Plus it was only the one time." Though today had been an invitation for more.

His sister offered a saccharine smile. "If you two didn't think we picked up on your stripping each other with your eyes in that meeting, you really don't have a clue."

"It's unwise. We're CEO and COO. The board—"

"The board can kiss my ass," she said. "This is our company. The Knoxes. The Thompsons. If you're happy—and you can make her happy—who the hell cares what anyone thinks?"

It was as good as having her blessing. He'd had good reasons to be careful, but Gia was right. Who the hell cared what anyone thought?

"You're thinking about it, and I don't want to be around while that happens. Later, bro." Gia headed to the elevator, waving without turning around.

When Royce entered his office, Taylor Thompson was sitting primly on the edge of his desk, her long legs crossed, one red stiletto wiggling in the air. Her devil-may-care smile paired with red lipstick was enough to send him falling at her feet and selling his very soul for one more kiss. One more touch. One more chance to blow her mind.

He wasn't typically led around by his pecker, but here they were. He'd known what he was doing in that meeting. Despite the excuses he gave Gia, the decision to seduce Taylor was cemented in his mind.

"What have we here?" He closed the door behind him, noticing the shades had been pulled. He pushed the lock on the doorknob. It engaged with an audible click.

"Your power's gone to my head." She was still wiggling that foot. He caught her calf in one palm and smoothed his hand over the muscle and down, down, until he pulled her shoe off and dropped it on the floor.

"Same." Repeating the action with her other foot, he said, "You told Gia."

"I...did," she admitted.

"I'm beginning to wonder if I don't care what anyone thinks."

"You cared enough to lock that door." Her cocked eyebrow was a challenge. He ended the stance with his lips on hers, drinking her in. His thirst had been unquenchable this week. When he'd seen her in the hallways talking with Bran or Addison, he'd felt a pinch in his chest he'd been sure was a warning to stay away. But when the lights went down in the meeting he recognized it for what it was.

Want.

A truckload of it.

Touching her hadn't relieved the urge. No. Touching her had been a lit match set to the driest kindling. He'd gone up in smoke and it'd taken everything in him not to pleasure her right there in the damn meeting, teasing her folds with his fingers until his lips could finish the job.

She unbuttoned his shirt, leaving his bow tie knotted at his collar and kissing his bare chest. He caught her head, enjoying the heat of her mouth on his skin.

One night hadn't been enough.

There was no erasing kisses that might as well have been burned into his flesh. She'd consumed him that night, reminding him what real passion felt like—not appreciation, not accomplishment, but real passion for another human being. The gut-shaking, teeth-rattling *need* to bury himself to the hilt, growling her name as he guided her to the pinnacle.

In a matter of seconds, he had her dress unzipped, his hands on her bare breasts, her bra tossed over his computer screen. She returned the favor by opening his pants and gripping his hard-as-steel cock.

She continued what he started in that meeting and he was going to finish it.

Right now.

He dragged his office chair to the side of the desk where she perched. He sat and lowered the chair to the lowest possible height, which brought him eye level with her delicious center.

"What are you doing?" Her voice held jittery notes of excitement.

"Three guesses," he said before pulling off her underwear—a red thong, God help him.

Legs parted, she dropped back onto her elbows and rested her calves on his shoulders. Giving his neglected member a squeeze, he promised to take care of it later. After he kissed his way along Taylor's thighs until he reached the Promised Land.

Oh hell yes.

Not only did she taste as incredible as he'd imagined, but her citrusy smell surrounded him. Her thighs clamped around his ears rendered him deaf save for the sound of her fingers raking through his hair and her sultry moans making a new home in his chest.

He used everything he'd learned about women to please her, sweeping his tongue left and right, up and down, flicking fast and laying it flat and then going slow. As a result, his lemon-scented vixen was having trouble keeping quiet, which made him grin in arrogant male pride.

"How you doin' up there?" he paused to ask but didn't wait for her to answer. Instead he set the pace with his tongue as he tugged her plush hips forward on the desk. He paused only briefly. To say: "Come for me, Taylor."

He wasn't sure if the request worked, but her orgasm followed. Then he was tasting her essence, luxuriating in her sighs of pleasure. She lost her place, writhing and sweeping the phone off the desk. It landed with a clatter that still didn't pull her from her bliss. Another wave hit and she clutched a paper in her hands, crumpling it as her other hand pushed his calculator and his glasses case to the floor.

He eased his mouth away, kissing his way down her legs and lingering at the back of one of her knees. He kissed along her calf and down to her feet, where he gave her big toe a playful lick.

When she sat up her blond hair was wild, her eyes wilder. He was enamored by the sheer wonder of her.

She was as unpredictable as a lightning storm and twice as dangerous. And here he was out in an open field, umbrella held high. With her, he never knew where he was headed. He'd left the black-and-white world of his making and was now wandering in the haze-gray fog of hers.

But there was no erasing what was happening between them. They were best when they were naked together. Even with no time or inclination for a serious relationship, he recognized his physical need for her. It was undeniable. *She* was undeniable.

The tent building behind his boxer briefs as she lowered to her knees in front of him was only partial proof. He rested a hand on her head and she slicked his length and took him into her mouth.

That genie he'd sworn to stuff back into the bottle? Yeah, that wasn't happening. Not when Taylor made his pulse race and his mind blank. Not when she made everything, at least in this moment, feel undeniably, inexplicably *right*.

Fifteen

Taylor always wanted a fireplace in the bedroom, but her apartment didn't have that particular feature. Nor did it have stone floors, Tuscan-style decor or a California king-size bed.

Royce's house did.

She stretched beneath the downy bedding, gold and red, and watched the flames. After another week of barely containing themselves at work, tonight made the third—no, wait, *fourth*—night they'd given in to what they both wanted. He'd come to her house yesterday with takeout. They ate after they'd satisfied another hunger: the one for each other. She'd enjoyed five-star cuisine naked and while lounging in front of the television.

Tonight wasn't dissimilar, though they ate dinner

first—and in public—before returning to Royce's house and promptly shedding their clothing. She'd had no idea how domestic he was, in spite of knowing him half her life. But since hanging out with him in his house and hers, she'd seen him cook—scrambled eggs counted—tidy up and, like now, deliver drinks.

He entered the room with a tray holding a bottle of scotch and two glasses. She knew the brand. It was her father's favorite when he was alive.

"I had my first taste of scotch with your dad." Royce placed the tray between them on the wide bed. He wore nothing but black boxer briefs, which had officially stolen the number one spot as her favorite outfit on him. The suit and bow tie combo had been her favorite for years, but oh, how wrong she'd been.

"I was eighteen. Just graduated high school." He handed her a lowball. A few inches of brown liquid surrounded a square ice cube that was almost the same size as the glass. "And a cigar."

"Sounds like Dad."

"Charlie pulled me aside and said, 'Now that you're a man, you should drink and smoke like one.'" Royce's smile was warm. "Never took to the cigars. But I do like the drink. The smoky, complicated nature of it."

"Sounds like you," she teased.

"I thought we'd toast to him."

Her eyes misted over. "You know."

"That today is his birthday? Yes. I know."

"I hate it. Scotch." She sat up, awkwardly covering

her naked breasts with the blanket while trying not to spill the drink. "But I'll have it in Dad's honor."

Her nose wrinkled as the liquid streamed down her throat in a trail of fire.

"Ugh. Still terrible," she wheezed. She'd never liked scotch, though she tried to build up a tolerance after her father passed. She'd wanted to feel closer to him and thought that might suffice. No such luck.

"Here." She offered her glass to Royce. "You drink it."

"It's there. The appreciation for it. Go slow. Let it open up. Just take it a sip at a time."

His advice was a good metaphor for them. The appreciation for Royce had been one taste at a time. He'd been slow to open up, too. That first all-in kiss had rocked her world—it was too much at once. After another "sip" of him, he'd easily become an addiction.

They'd given in to the "more" between them. First with sex in his office, then this week where they were behaving like a… Dare she say it? *Couple*.

There was no bridge being burned if they didn't work out. He would return to work as usual and she would make herself forget that the best sex of her life was courtesy of the man she worked closely with every day.

Then again, if things worked out…

The thought made her smile. Her next sip of scotch went down easier than the first.

"The ice helps." Royce was lounging on the padded headboard, a pillow behind his back. He watched the fire but she couldn't take her eyes off his face.

The orange glow highlighting a strong, straight nose and angled jaw. The kissable firmness of his lips, and his regal eyebrows.

"Dad trusted me to follow in his footsteps," she said. "My being COO is a tribute to him in a lot of ways."

"But?" Royce tilted his head, reading her tone correctly.

"But, I also wanted a family. My mother never believed that work and family can coexist."

His expression blanked, but he kept the conversation going. "What do you think?"

"I believe I can have it all." She watched her drink, not wanting him to think she was talking about him when she added, "A husband. A family. A career. But I worry about balance. About one area suffering while the other excels."

"Balance is hard," he agreed in the same noncommittal tone.

"My father was all about his career, but still made time for me. He took me to work with him on more than one occasion."

"I remember."

"You do?" She recalled seeing Royce at Thom-Knox fresh out of college, when she was a teenager. She had no idea he'd noticed her beyond the moment he caught her in his arms. And then she'd been pretty sure it hadn't registered as an event worth remembering to him.

"He told me to stay away from you," Royce said now.

"Dad?" She'd been lectured but had no idea that he'd gone to Royce, too. "Wow. That's embarrassing."

"It was necessary." He raked his eyes over her body, then touched a nipple that peeked out from the sheet. "Look where we've ended up."

She had to smile, though the news that he was told to stay away from her rocked her where she sat. "My father had a lot of nerve."

"He loved you."

"He was ten years older than my mom, did you know that? And they were great together. Why didn't he think I could handle a relationship with you?" She sensed she was treading on sacred ground. That her father's reasons had been buried with him.

Royce didn't seem to think so. "If I had to guess, I'd say it was stereotypical fatherly protection. He was my age once, and had your mother in his sights. Do you believe he was always the consummate gentleman?"

"Ew." But she had to laugh. Her parents had been very much in love, and Deena was gorgeous. No doubt her father's thoughts about her were less than wholesome. "He liked Brannon for me."

"A safer choice."

She could hear the pride in his voice at being the *forbidden choice*. Bran and Taylor had never had the kind of explosive attraction that Royce and Taylor had.

"Don't be so hard on him," Royce told her. "Your father couldn't bear the idea of you growing up. He could have acted out of self-preservation that had nothing to do with us. God knows my father's done that."

"Jack knows how to draw attention, that's for sure."

Royce watched the fire, silent.

"When we talked about you being named CEO, you said it was your responsibility." She rattled the oversize ice cube in her glass. "Was that all it was?"

"It's my legacy. My birthright. Just as COO is yours. Your dad only wanted the best for you, Taylor. Whatever he said or did while he was here, he said or did with you in mind. You meant everything to him."

"I miss him." She hugged the glass to her chest. A poor substitute for her dad. There would always be a void in her arms.

"So do I." Royce sat his glass aside, gathered her close and kissed the top of her head.

"How did my mom lose him and remain standing?" she asked, not expecting an answer. He didn't offer one, consoling her with a hand moving up and down along her arm. "Is the reward for finally finding *The One* losing them in the end? How is that fair?"

"Losing people we love is par for the course, Taylor. None of us get out of this life alive. Someone always has to go first."

As sad as his words were, they were oddly comforting. She snuggled into him.

"Something I'm learning," he murmured. He touched the bottom of the glass she still cradled. Her next sip was smoother than the last. "Well?"

"Complex," she answered. It was a good way to describe scotch.

Complex was also a good way to describe the feelings she was developing for Royce. She hadn't thought about The End, not really, but she considered, ever so briefly, the beauty of being someone's forever.

"We have to stop meeting like this." Taylor stepped into the supply closet attached to the copy room. It'd been five days since she sipped scotch in Royce's bed. Five days since he held her in his arms and consoled her. Five days since she realized her feelings for him were deepening.

She'd been trying not to focus on those "feelings," since feelings were fickle. But she couldn't keep from walking toward the glow of the supply closet—especially when the silhouette inside belonged to suited, bow-tied Royce.

He'd been working a lot this week, and late. Tonight was no exception. The executive floor was practically abandoned at this hour. She understood his new position was demanding. This was a temporary state—the shift from one position to the other wouldn't last forever. Soon he could go home before nine at night.

They hadn't had much time together this week and she missed it. Missed *him*, in spite of working with him every single day. When he was with her, he was warm. Open. In the previous weeks, she'd caught a glimpse of who he could be if he weren't shackled to ThomKnox, but that version of him had gone the way of the brontosaurus.

"You're working late."

He looked exhausted—from the shadows beneath his eyes to the rumpled look of his usually starched shirt. "I can't find anything in here." He picked up a box of staples. "I was looking for those clamp things."

"Sounds kinky."

He gave her a tired smile.

She reached behind him for a box of black binder clips. "These?"

"Yes." He took the box. "Thank you. Assistant interviews are killing me. Half the candidates list video games as their past experience and the other half are wildly overqualified. Finding the right person from those two piles is a challenge. No wonder Bran sings Addison's praises all the time."

"You'll find the right one." She fingered the red bow tie at his collar. "In the meantime, how lucky that I stumbled across you in a closet."

"Role reversal of the Valentine's gala." Heat replaced the fatigue in his eyes. He wanted her. Just like that. Nice to know their physical attraction hadn't dampened.

She kissed his frown and his lips softened against hers, the box of binder clips rattling as he wrapped his arms around her and pulled her closer. She raked her fingers into his hair, moaning when his tongue touched hers. She'd never tire of that move.

"How wrong is it to have sex in this closet?" she whispered.

His grin was slow, wicked. "Well, I *am* in charge now."

"Mmm, don't I know it." She let her hands roam

while he made out with her long and slow, his movements languid. She guessed he needed to shake off the long-and-turning-longer week, and so did she. No sense in wasting an opportunity to blow off some steam—and each other's minds.

Suddenly, a light flipped on in the copy room, illuminating the shadowed pocket of the supply closet.

"Oh! Sorry, I…" Addison stood, papers in hand, obviously en route to the copy machine. "Oh. My God."

But her *Oh. My. God.* sounded pleasantly surprised rather than accusatory. Taylor unwound her arms from Royce's neck. His hands moved to her hips and he positioned himself behind her. The thick ridge of his erection nestled against her bottom. She would've smiled if she wasn't concerned about Addison's reaction.

If Addi didn't know about Taylor and Royce, she did now. And if Brannon had any leftover doubts about them, one conversation with his assistant would erase them.

"I'll take care of this later." Addison sent them another glance before turning to leave the copy room.

"Addi, wait." Taylor followed Addi to the doorway. There was a distance between them that Taylor didn't like. It niggled at her that Bran's assistant thought of Taylor as "the bad guy." Taylor didn't like being *unliked* by anyone.

"Yes?" Addison faced her.

"You've been upset with me lately. I might be

speaking out of turn, but I feel like it has something
to do with Brannon."

Addison's cheeks turned bold pink, but she didn't
confirm nor deny.

"I don't know what you heard, but Bran never actually proposed to me. He and I decided we were better
off friends. Mutually. That hug you saw—"

"Was none of my business. Honestly, Taylor, this
is unnecessary."

"You look at Brannon like…" *The way I used to
look at Royce.* "Like you're interested in more. Does
he know how you feel about him?"

"I—I don't understand what this is about. If it's
discretion you're after, you can trust me not to say
anything about you and Royce."

"No, that's not it. You and Bran—"

"Have a professional relationship, not a personal
one." Addison's smile was plastic. "Who you kiss at
work is none of my business. I'm just trying to do
my job."

Yowch.

Addison made it halfway down the corridor before Taylor decided to make one last ditch effort at
peace between them.

"I think you and Bran would be good together!"
she called out. "For what it's worth."

Addi stopped walking and turned her head slowly
to the side. She looked half mortified, half nauseous,
and then Taylor saw why.

Brannon entered the corridor slowly, his pained
expression and Addison's a matching set.

Taylor winced. The road to recovery for her and Addison was about to become even longer thanks to Taylor's big mouth…and the fact that Brannon heard every word that came out of it.

Sixteen

The journey from CFO to CEO wasn't going as smoothly as he'd originally—and naively—believed. Turned out the transition was more complicated than swapping the nameplate on his desk.

Royce was still responsible for his CFO duties while adjusting to CEO. Luckily he'd had a round of interviews today for CFO, and had met with two very promising prospects. He looked forward to finalizing the decision and offloading some of his work.

He'd managed to grab dinner with Taylor one night this week, a far cry from how many nights he preferred spending with her. She was understanding, and had mentioned to him that "these things" took time before reassuring him his hectic schedule was temporary.

"It'll work out. You'll see," she'd said.

Comforting words, but harder in practice than in theory.

He'd promised to leave the office by noon on Thursday to meet her for lunch—just like he'd promised on Friday. And today. His entire week had been derailed and here he was on a Saturday having missed yet another opportunity to see her.

He picked up his cell phone to text an apology when she appeared in the doorway of his office holding a brown sack with handles.

"Surprise!"

He took one look at the familiar black logo on the bag, one whiff of the enticing smells of garlic, robust tomato sauce and rich oregano, and his stomach roared.

"That smells incredible," were his first words. "As do you." Her wide smile suggested she didn't mind that he'd complimented the food before her.

"I didn't hear from you at noon."

He checked his cell phone for the time. 1:47 p.m.? "I'm sorry. I was going to call. I had no idea how late it was."

"I figured. I had to come into the office and check on a few things, anyway." She glanced at the stacks of paper on his desk that had spilled from his inbox. "You know, you could ask for my help."

He gestured to the eleven windows open on his computer screen. "And subject you to this? I like you too much."

"Who else can you trust with the company's biggest secrets?" She unloaded their lunch onto the low table in front of a pair of guest chairs. She offered a hunk of ciabatta bread and his mouth watered. Garlic was his favorite contemporary Italian restaurant in River Grove. The yeasty, warm bread was a gluten-free person's worst nightmare. He opened the lid on a container. A huge square of lasagna covered in freshly grated Parmesan cheese caused his stomach to rumble again.

"You're serious?" He dunked the bread into the sauce and took a bite. Heavenly.

"I *am* COO. I can handle some of the excess in the short term. Plus us working closely solves the problem of finding time to see each other. Sort of like date-working." She handed him a plastic fork.

"Scandalous."

"For two of the top brass at ThomKnox, it very well might be." She smiled.

He kissed the corner of that smile. They ate, discussing strategy and how some of his workload could be pieced and parceled out. By the time she stuffed their empty food containers into the bag—he'd helped finish her eggplant parmesan, which he begrudgingly admitted was better than anticipated—he was alive with the excitement of having a plan.

"How's Bran doing?" she asked out of nowhere.

He ignored the rogue spike of jealousy. Royce knew Taylor wanted to be with him, not his brother— her reaction on Valentine's Day had solidified that— so him feeling possessive over her made no sense.

"Bran's busy ignoring me."

"I don't know why he's mad at you. Your father picked you to be CEO. It's not as if you lobbied for it."

He tucked her dark blond hair behind her ear. "It's more about my not telling Bran when I knew. I should've."

"You didn't know Jack was going to announce it at the party." But her tone held a question she spoke when she said, "Did you?"

"I didn't know. But I could've guessed." His father liked the spotlight and he'd much rather go out with a bang than a fizzle.

"You're sure about taking on some of the workload while I'm finding an assistant?" He tipped her chin.

"I'm sure."

"Thank you. And thank you…for the other things."

"Other things?"

"You breezed in here, fed me and took my stress away."

"Yeah, but I was just—"

He kissed her gently, enjoying when she went pliant beneath him. He'd had a hell of a week and having her support meant a lot to him. Even if it was hard to admit he needed it. "I appreciate it. More than you know. That's what I'm trying to say."

He was in undiscovered territory. Having someone to rely on, to trust, had been absent from his personal life for a long time. Taylor made him feel more capable, not less. Having her in his corner was an idea he was already used to.

As long as he kept work first and wasn't distracted,

he didn't see the harm. ThomKnox was his number one focus. There wasn't room for much more.

"This feels like an abuse of power." Taylor bit her lip and stared at the curtly worded email on the screen.

"Why?"

She narrowed her eyelids. "You know why. Lowell Olsen is a huge distributor and you're willing to ruin the relationship because I don't like him?"

"No one likes him. Plus, he's bullying you. We don't negotiate with bullies. We'll find a better store."

She hesitated over her laptop keyboard. "But—"

His finger on top of hers, he pressed a button and the "we're no longer interested in placing ThomKnox merchandise in your store" email was sent.

"Oh my gosh. You didn't!" She was elated and shocked and almost—fine, she'd admit it—*drunk with power*.

"I did. And now it's done."

As romantic gestures went, this wasn't hearts and flowers, or chocolates and a puppy wearing a big red bow. But Royce's love language was work. Roughly translated, his ending negotiations with Lowell Olsen felt romantic to her.

She supposed that was expected from a woman in love.

Yep. She'd done it. She'd fallen head over heels for Royce Knox. Of course, she knew better than to share that with him. He'd been buried up to his eyeballs since he'd been appointed CEO and was only now treading water and breathing at the same time. A profession of true love on top of that might send him over the edge.

He took the laptop from her and set it on a pile of papers, mail and folders on the coffee table. "Guess what?"

You love me, too?

"What?"

"Time for dessert."

"Dessert?" They'd shared a very unsexy dinner of pizza and more pizza. It might've been goat cheese and pear with smoked, caramelized onion sauce, but it was still pizza and she'd eaten a ton of it. "How could you be hungry for anything after…" She trailed off as he reached for the waistband of her leggings and began tugging them from her legs. "Royce."

"Dessert," he insisted. "You've worked very hard this weekend and you deserve a reward."

How could she argue with that? She couldn't. Not when he urged her to her back and peeled those pants the rest of the way off. Or when he kissed her belly button, down her thighs and then up to her—*oh*.

His tongue should be bronzed. He was that good.

The skills he had in the boardroom were super-sized in the bedroom—or the living room. In any room. She'd been sleeping with him for a little over a month and he'd never failed to render her a bone-less mass, her blood sizzling and popping like oil in a hot pan. The man *was* sex, and she couldn't reconcile how well he'd kept the friskier part of himself hidden from her—from the world. Who knew *this* was lurking beneath the veneer of a serious, sometimes-bespectacled number cruncher.

"Yes, *there*," she encouraged, her mind blanking as he tasted her.

"How about *here*?"

She liked to think she'd coaxed out his inner sexy beast. After all, he'd brought out the animal in her. Could she be his secret superpower? Was Royce hers? He knew what she needed physically and had never failed to deliver. She'd been exactly who he needed whether at work or at home. Helping him hadn't been charity; it'd come naturally. The way a couple in love prioritized being there for each other.

Royce's second finger joined his first in the race to her orgasm. Her hips bucked as she tumbled over in record time. Static fuzz descended, blotting out her worries. The words on her tongue as she clutched around his fingers were "Yes, Royce, yes." But if the timing had been different, if she would've allowed her heart to speak for her, those words would have been *"I love you. I love you..."*

In a perfect world, he would've returned that sentiment instead of saying, "Be right back."

As he left the room, she warned herself not to rush him. She wanted him however she could have him, and if that meant she loved him with everything in her without him knowing, then that's how it would have to be. They had plenty of time for him to realize he loved her, too. He had a lot on his plate. That was all.

He returned to the living room, sheathed, but instead of crashing down over her, he lifted her into his arms. Pressing her back against the nearest blank wall, he instructed her to wrap her legs around his waist.

She did as she was told and was rewarded by the long, slick slide of him entering her. Sensitive from his earlier kisses, her channel tightened around him as he moved, giving them both the pressure they desired.

"Taylor. *God.*" Each broken word fell from lips she kissed over and over, while her fingers toyed in his hair. She kept her gaze on his face, her truncated breaths sawing from her lungs as they made love against the wall. She had to see the moment he came. Had to witness taking him over the edge of control— control he favored but relinquished whenever he was with her.

It was heady, that power shift.

His hips sped and sweat broke out on his forehead. Loud groans of excitement exited his throat, folded around swear words.

"Harder. Harder," she encouraged. *I love you.*

"I'm there. I'm there." His voice faded into a shout of completion as he pressed her back flat against the wall. She absorbed his weight and strength, kissing his face and neck and tasting the salt on his skin.

He loved her, too. Soon he'd realize it. She wouldn't rush him.

They had plenty of time.

Seventeen

A quick *rap-rap-rap* echoed off Royce's office door but his visitor didn't wait to be invited before opening it.

"I'm not *not* speaking to you." Brannon walked in and shut the door behind him.

Royce pulled his glasses off his nose. "Good. Now get out. I'm busy." He figured Brannon had been keeping busy, too. Their stint of not talking, of not hanging out would end eventually. Even if it had been nearly a month since the meeting where Gia asked about their "snit."

She'd come into Royce's office last week telling him if he hurt Taylor, she'd castrate him. He told her it wasn't serious, which was a bold-faced lie. Not only had Taylor and Royce been sleeping together for six weeks, he'd seen her several times last week and twice this week alone. And they had plans tonight.

As for Bran, he knew that Royce and Taylor were "dating," but that was also a tame way to describe their relationship. Royce had yet to clue his brother in on any details. Not that he'd asked.

"If you're going to insist on staying, at least sit down," Royce told him.

"Why don't you stand?"

"Because I'm working. Didn't we just cover this?"

"We have an appointment at noon." Bran folded his arms over his chest, defiant.

"I have no such appointment on my calendar."

"Write one in and get off your ass. Let's go."

"If you have something to say, why don't you say it and then go back to what you were doing before you came in here to interrupt me with this nonsense?"

"This 'nonsense' is exactly why we're not speaking. And this appointment is one you need to show up for. It's what's going to put us back where we belong."

Royce would do anything for his brother, including going to a mystery appointment so that they could make amends. They *needed* to make amends. They had a company to run—ThomKnox wouldn't function with two out of three Knox siblings. Success required all of them.

He shut his laptop and stood from his chair. "What do I need to bring?"

Bran's smile was smug. "You don't need to bring anything. I have it covered."

* * *

Bran's house was a sleek, modern, square utopia. Glass and steel and clean lines made up the design; none of the homier accents like bowls of fruit or vases of flowers here. Odd the way the architecture of Royce's and Bran's homes contrasted the men themselves—Royce's love of spreadsheets and black-and-white areas should have made him better suited to sparse decor. Outside, a huge patio area outfitted with a bar and seating flanked an in-ground pool and a new feature to the yard—one that fit Bran to a T.

"Is that…?" Royce started.

"A boxing ring."

"So you took Dad seriously."

"I figured it'd be good exercise. I've been practicing with the trainer. Know what I noticed?"

"You're no Mike Tyson?" Royce answered drily.

"I noticed that it helps release emotion." Bran pulled on one boxing glove and then threw Royce a pair. "It resolves issues that were formerly unresolved."

"I'm not going to fight you, Bran."

"It's not fighting. It's boxing. It's a sport."

This was ridiculous. What did he hope to solve with the two of them throwing punches?

"What's wrong? Afraid I'll kick your ass?" Bran offered a crooked smile.

Even as Royce assured himself he had nothing to prove to his younger brother, he was baited by that challenge. Giving in to his baser instincts, he tossed his suit jacket aside and pulled his boxing gloves on as well.

After the quickest tutorial ever, Royce and Bran began circling each other in the ring.

"You should've told me Dad chose you," Bran said.

"He asked me not to." Royce held his arms wide.

"Gloves up. I don't want to break your nose." Bran demonstrated by shielding his own face.

"This is stupid." But Royce put his gloves up. He liked his nose the way it was, thank you very much.

"We're in this together, big brother. That means circumventing Dad sometimes. Like when we broke the window in the guest bedroom and moved a plant in front of it instead of telling him what happened."

"We didn't get away with that, either." Bouncing on the balls of his feet, Royce lifted his gloves in time to thwart an incoming swing.

"Good block. That doesn't change the fact that I would've liked to know what you knew. Rather than sit there with my dick in my hand at the party."

"Pretty sure all eyes were on me. Which I didn't appreciate, you know."

"We could've been a unified front." Bran swiped the air, but Royce ducked out of the way.

"Nothing above the neck, remember? Those were the rules."

"They're more like guidelines." Bran danced in a half circle. "How are you and Taylor doing?"

"What?"

"Don't play coy with me. You and Taylor have been all over each other lately. Beyond the one time Addison caught you in the supply closet, I'm assuming." Bran took another swing and, thankfully, missed. "Didn't suspect you for the falling-in-love type."

"What are you—" Royce dropped his gloves but lifted them just as fast to block a blow meant for his jaw.

Bran laughed, enjoying himself way too much. "Keep your guard up!"

"What are we, teenagers? I'm not *falling in love*. Taylor and I are partners in the most physical sense of the word."

"She doesn't want any more from you?"

Her words from the night they'd shared scotch came back to him. "She wants a family and marriage, but she also wants a career. I'm certain I'm only involved in the last part of that list."

"How certain?"

Royce stilled, giving his brother an impatient glare.

"You're smart, Royce, but dense when it comes to women."

Royce threw a punch and missed, but knocked Bran's footing off. That felt good.

"You're one to talk," he told his younger brother. "Addison wants you and you're a clueless oaf."

"Taylor embarrassed us both when she shouted that we'd be good together. The whole office heard."

"The four of us were the only ones in the office."

"Yeah, well, Addi and I are coworkers *in the most physical sense of the word*. Stop changing the subject."

A few more swings were thrown, but none of them

connected. Bran's comments circled Royce's head like a school of hungry piranha.

"What do you know about Taylor, anyway?" Royce finally asked, wondering if Bran was dancing around a point as well as this boxing ring.

"She's been my friend most of her life," Bran answered. "She's always talked about having kids, a husband. A golden retriever, for Christ's sake. That doesn't sound anything like you."

It didn't. But that was never what Royce and Taylor were about.

"Name the flower she's allergic to," Bran said.

"Daisies." It was a guess. Royce swung, aiming for Bran's ribs. His brother slid out of the way, easy as you please. His trainer was good.

"Lilies." Bran smirked. "Do you talk to her, ever?"

Grunting as he stepped out of the way of one of Bran's throws, Royce said, "We must've skipped over that all-important 'do you or don't you like lilies' conversation so crucial to new couples."

"So you admit you're a couple now." Bran stopped moving. Royce threw another punch, but landed against the ropes when his forward momentum took him there.

"I'm sure you two had a lot more time to talk than she and I do." Royce pushed off the ropes, spun on his brother and swung. The punch connected. Bran clutched his stomach and let out an audible *oof.*

Satisfied, Royce added, "We use our mouths for other pastimes when we're together."

Bran turned and landed the hit he'd been angling

for since they stepped into the ring. Light exploded behind Royce's eye and he held up his glove a millisecond too late.

"What the hell!" Royce cupped his eye, which was beginning to feel the same size as his boxing glove.

"Sorry. That was supposed to be your nose," Bran said, not sounding sorry at all.

"What's this about? Do you want her for yourself or something?" Dammit, his eye hurt.

Bran dropped his arms, gloves hanging at his sides, a look of utter surprise on his face. "That's history. You know that, right? Taylor and I patched up what almost happened—what would've been a disaster. This has nothing to do with me trying to win the girl."

"So you're pissed I won CEO and you didn't?" Royce's head hadn't begun to throb yet but he guessed it would start any second.

"No. Goddammit, Royce. I'm pissed you didn't trust Gia or me with that news. We've always been a unit. *Always*."

Royce heard the hurt in his brother's voice. What he said was true. Bran and Gia and Royce were three members of a busy, hardworking family. They were far from latchkey kids, but considering that a staff cared for them during the busy early years of Thom-Knox, the three siblings leaned on each other first and foremost.

Bran tore off his gloves. "Taylor Thompson is in love with you, and if you don't see that, you're a bigger idiot than I was." He ducked between the ropes and sat on the steps leading out of the ring.

Royce scrunched his face, aware of the dull thud of a bruise forming. A shiner for the new CEO. *Great.* He stepped out of the ring and joined Bran, whose elbows were resting on his knees.

"I messed up, Royce," Bran said to his shoes. Both of them were panting from their workout.

Royce took a clumsy step, regained his balance and sat next to his brother. "Your heart was in the right place."

"That's just it. My heart wasn't involved at all." Bran sighed. "If you tell anyone this I'll black your other eye."

Royce held up a hand and silently swore his allegiance.

"I thought being engaged to Taylor would give me a better shot at CEO."

Royce frowned. "You're plenty qualified for CEO."

"Yeah, I know. But I wasn't an option in Dad's eyes. It was you the whole time. Part of me knew that. And when you knew that, I wish you would have come to me so that we could've had a moment to absorb it away from all those extra sets of eyes."

Royce's shoulders dropped. He wished that, too.

"I could've hurt Taylor, Royce. She didn't love me, but if she had and I led her on?" Bran shook his head. "She never would've forgiven me for backing out of our engagement. And I would've backed out eventually. I care about her, but marriage? That's insane."

Just hearing the word *marriage* in reference to

Taylor made the hair on Royce's neck stand on end. "I doubt she wants to marry me." But his voice wasn't as solid as he'd like it to be. They'd grown close. Shared a lot of intimate nights and slept side by side. She'd brought him lunch and offered to help him at work and, like he'd pointed out a few minutes ago, they were a new couple.

Couple.

He sure as hell wasn't ready for that.

"Next time you talk to Taylor, do me a favor and let her know that Addi and I are not going to date each other."

"Why not? Addison's pretty."

"Pretty? She's gorgeous. But if Taylor keeps teasing her, Addi might quit. You know how hard it is to find a good assistant." Bran was shaking his head again, more adamantly than before. "I rounded the corner after Taylor shouted we'd be good together, and Addi looked like she wanted the floor to swallow her. Trust me, the only thing between Ad and me is professional compatibility. If she liked me, I'd know it."

"Don't be so sure. Not every woman who likes you jumps you in a closet."

Bran crashed into Royce and tumbled him off the steps and into the plush grass, but he was laughing when he did it. The backyard scuffle reminded Royce of the few times they'd wrestled as kids. Never fighting to win anything, always on the same side. Like now.

Bran collapsed next to him, his back to the ground.

"I'm sorry I didn't tell you about CEO," Royce said. "I should have."

"Yeah. Don't do it again."

Royce let out a small chuckle, then fell silent. They lay side by side for a moment, their eyes on the bright blue sky overhead. Royce's head was thumping hard enough to outrace his heart. Partially because of the eye, partially because he knew what he had to do when it came to Taylor.

The position of CEO was rewarding, but demanding. Taylor had been in second place since he accepted the position, and he'd believed that she was okay with it. Now he wondered if that was the case. Would she eventually expect more than he had the ability to give? Did she already expect more?

Bran was right. The Knox trio had always been a unit. He owed his brother and sister the courtesy of *not* tanking their family legacy. Hell, he'd swung the felling blow to keep their products out of retail establishments that might've contributed to a significant percentage of sales. Why? Because he'd wanted to please Taylor.

It was time to stop playing house and focus on work—only work.

His chest howled in protest. He wanted her. God, how he wanted her. In his bed, in his life. On his couch. *On my desk.* But when it came to giving her what she ultimately desired—a family—he had no idea when he'd be ready. If he'd *ever* be ready.

His future was predetermined. The success of ThomKnox rested squarely on his shoulders.

Eighteen-hour days wouldn't leave much room for Taylor. She'd accepted his wacky schedule so far, but what about in six months? A year? His dream was coming true, but how long should she wait to have hers? He refused to be the man who would always be telling her, "Let's wait another year…"

His dreams were important, but so were hers. He and Taylor had the physical attraction on lock, but where it counted—when building a life came into the picture, how could he ask her to table her wants and needs for him?

"I smell your brain cooking," Bran said, hands on his own chest and eyes turned toward Royce. "Thinking hard?"

"You might've knocked some sense into me."

"You're welcome." Bran stood, his lighter brown hair highlighted in a halo around his head, part of it falling over his forehead as he looked down. "You need ice."

"You need a haircut."

Bran would probably brag to everyone that he was responsible for the black eye. Just what Royce needed. Bran toed Royce in the ribs and then headed inside. Royce stayed on his back, listening as the icemaker rattled out the cubes that would soon soothe his aching head.

He knew what he had to do when it came to Taylor.

But he didn't want to do it.

Eighteen

No time like the present.

Royce didn't know if flowers were the right accompaniment for what he'd come to say, but he couldn't show up empty-handed for this conversation. He was glad Bran mentioned Taylor's lily allergy. Royce had been sure not to include a single one of them in the bouquet.

His eyes were grainy, his stomach upset—in part due to the decision he felt forced to make, and in part due to the coffee he'd drunk to wake up. He hadn't slept well last night. He'd been awake turning over his and Taylor's relationship. CEO and ThomKnox. Brannon's advice. Gia, and even Jayson Cooper. Gia and Coop had been so in love they'd stunk with it.

So in love they made everyone around them roll their eyes. Then they were over.

In a blink.

If a couple like Gia and Jayson could implode when they had true love on their side, what chance did Royce and Taylor have? If he didn't end things with her now—if they continued to blend their individual dreams and it didn't work out—Taylor would grow to resent him. Conversations about family or work would be riddled with landmines. They'd argue. Say things they didn't mean. They'd end in a nuclear-bomb-worthy plume of smoke. He didn't want that.

He wanted her to have a perfect life—a future that she chose, not one that was a compromise. He cared about her—she was practically family—and if there was a chance for her to escape unscathed, he would do what had to be done… While they could still blame proximity and timing on their attraction.

If she was in love at all, it was with the idea of him. Not him. He knew that. But he also appreciated how the lines could blur when sexual attraction was at its peak. Those moments after an orgasm had thrummed through his body like a power line, and he'd definitely felt something intense.

The heart was a tricky mistress, though. He couldn't allow emotion to cloud the surmountable tasks before him. The product launch. CEO. His retiring father. His brother and his sister depended on him. ThomKnox as a whole, including Taylor, depended on him. He didn't take that lightly.

He knew numbers and the math didn't work out

when he added Taylor and him together. He couldn't nurture both his job and his personal life. Not right now. Maybe in ten years, but how could he ask her to table what she wanted for *a decade*?

A family. A dog. And, he guessed, a husband who came home before ten o'clock at night after a grueling day at the office.

Obviously, he could provide financial stability and a warm bed—they sure as hell had a good time together—but juggling family responsibilities? His own father was loving, but hadn't often been present. He'd brought Royce to work with him, and then Bran. And then Gia. One might argue they were a part of this company because ThomKnox was where their family congregated. Other than Sunday breakfasts, Royce didn't recall a family vacation where his father hadn't been on the phone taking business calls.

Taylor's father hadn't been that way. He'd worked hard, but he'd also doted on her. Her mother had been equally enamored with her daughter and eventually left ThomKnox to be at home with her. Taylor wanted the best of both worlds—the job, the family. How had she put it? Balance.

Not his forte.

What if he *never* wanted a family? What if he was content to be CEO and run the company on his own? What if he was incapable of balance? He couldn't ask Taylor to lead half of a life. She'd already lost her father, and Royce wouldn't cost her her future family as well. He cared for her far too much—he could tell by the suffocating knot in his lungs. He cared for her more than he cared for himself, and that was why it was time to call this what it was.

An amazingly fun fling that was doomed from the start.

Flowers in hand, he swallowed down the bile pushing against the base of his throat. He'd never done anything this hard. Not ever. But he knew what he was capable of—and what he wasn't. The perks of being a practical numbers guy, he supposed. It was high time someone was honest about where he and Taylor stood.

The least he could do was be brave enough to say the words neither of them wanted to hear.

Taylor opened her front door and her breath caught. She admired the man on her stoop, easy to do when Royce looked so damn good. It was nice to see him here on a Saturday morning instead of at the office.

Weekends were for croissants and coffee and lounging in her leggings. Royce was a tad more formal in dark jeans. His button-down shirt was cuffed at the sleeves, revealing his tanned forearms. The bow tie was a nice touch. And sexy. Which she told him with a smile.

He didn't smile. He looked downright miserable, actually. She opened her mouth to ask him why, but he spoke before she could.

"You're allergic to lilies." He handed over the flower bouquet, a beautiful mix of daisies and roses interspersed with wildflowers she didn't recognize.

"I'm not allergic. But I don't particularly care for

them." She took a deep inhalation of the bouquet and stepped aside. "I love these. Thank you."

His frown only deepened. "Oh."

Clearly something was bothering him. Whatever had put that lost and lonely look in his eyes, they could handle it together. She loved him, and with loving someone came navigating the occasional bad day.

"Come in. I made sun tea."

"No, thank you." He didn't meet her eyes, regarding his shoes instead. A premonition skittered across her chest on eight hairy legs. "I'm not staying long."

"Okay." She stepped outside to join him, because even the scant distance between them at the threshold of her apartment was too much. He hadn't greeted her with a kiss, another change she'd noticed. That skittering hairy-legged creature climbed her spine.

"You want a family," Royce said in that same flat tone. Her mind scrambled. She wasn't sure where he was going with this, but the circles under his eyes told her it wasn't good. "Kids. House. A dog?"

"Yes. Um. Eventually." She crossed her arms over her chest. If he was about to break her heart, her folded arms were her only defense.

"That kiss in the closet at the gala changed my life," he said, his tone gentle. "The attraction between us was something neither of us could deny."

Relief came but was short-lived when he added, "I never intended for us to make it this far, or to embark on a relationship. Especially one where you're making plans with me... Plans I can't make with you."

"Royce, what are you talking about?" The flowers in her hands grew heavy, as if each soft petal was sculpted from concrete. She tossed the bouquet on the small chair on her stoop and wondered if she should've sat in the chair instead. Her knees weren't very stable at the moment.

"The tablet launch is happening soon." His words were robotic. Carefully measured. "My first big release as CEO. The hours I've been working are only going to increase."

"So will mine," she said with a half laugh. "It's only temporary."

"Like us."

Temporary.

She'd done the unthinkable: she'd fallen in love. Despite her telling herself not to do it, despite her justifications that she had plenty of time to win his heart.

"You're breaking up with me." Her words were as disconnected as if someone else had said them. She waited for him to refute that statement. Instead, he confirmed her worst fear.

"Yes. While we can still piece ourselves together. Before we end up like Gia and Jayson."

"What the hell does this have to do with Gia and Jayson?" She would love to know. She needed answers and didn't have any. Royce showing up at her apartment, delivering flowers and announcing that he didn't want her anymore had come out of nowhere. "What brought this on?"

"I had some sense knocked into me."

She'd noticed the dark bruise around his left eye. "Oh? Who do I have to thank for that?"

Royce said nothing.

"This isn't about Gia and Jayson," she said. "You didn't bring me flowers—" she shot a disgusted look at the gorgeous bouquet on the chair "—so that you could talk about your sister's failed marriage. Yes, I want a family. I told you that. *Eventually.* Not now."

"You never told me you fell in love with me." His tone was accusatory, and she instantly felt young and foolish, like she didn't know her own mind or her heart. Shame blanketed her like a heavy coat, and even in today's cooler temperature, she was suddenly too warm. Suffocating under the weight of this conversation. "I suspect you didn't tell me how you felt because you feared my reaction."

"I don't fear you at all." She was more afraid of herself. Or more accurately her emotions—the ones that had run ahead of her shouting, *Come on in! The water's fine!*

"You have a lot on your plate," she said, denial setting in. "You've been busy. *I've* been busy. I didn't want to distract you." But they were lame excuses. There'd been plenty of instances where she could've shared her feelings. She just…hadn't.

He was right. She didn't want to scare him away. She worried that putting pressure on him would cause him to shut down, like he was doing now.

"Nothing has to change," she said, desperate to make everything okay. "I'm trying to learn how to balance work and home life, too. We can figure it out together and—"

"How long?"

She blinked. "How long what?"

"How long are you willing to wait to start this family, Taylor? You're closing in on thirty. How long?"

"I don't know. A few years." She'd never had a conversation this intimate with anyone. Not with any guy she'd dated. And definitely not in front of her apartment where her neighbors could overhear.

"What about five years?" he asked. "How about seven? Ten?"

It took her a second to understand he wasn't negotiating. He was trying to prove a point.

"I won't ask you to design your life around me." Some of the hardness left his eyes. He was still in there, the man she fell in love with. The man who'd intrigued her for half her life. The man who'd caught her in his arms when she was too young to understand what her fluttering stomach meant was the same man who had thoroughly won her heart—only to demolish it now.

"Isn't that up to me?" she asked quietly.

"It's up to you and whomever you build a family with. My position as CEO reigns supreme over everything else. I won't be distracted from my legacy. I'm sorry, Taylor."

His apology was somehow more final than the whole of his breakup speech. His mind was made up. He was rejecting her.

It was like a bomb had gone off nearby and deafened her, leaving behind only a high-pitched ringing interspersed with her broken heartbeats.

Royce, task complete, walked to his car. She

watched him drive away, and only when he was out of sight did she sag against the door.

There was nothing to say after he'd said it all. He didn't have to say he didn't love her—he knew she loved him and had offered nothing in return. Except the assurance that ThomKnox mattered more than anything.

More than her.

Nineteen

Taylor's first instinct when Gia invited her to spend Sunday lounging at the pool was to answer with a definitive *no*.

She'd spent yesterday miserable and slept terribly on top of it. It was hard to achieve REM in between crying jags. She woke today grouchy and tired, and sad. So incredibly sad. The sadness reminded her of when her father passed away. It wasn't the same kind of grief, but it had the same depth. It choked the joy from her soul.

She'd thought of a million different ways she could've reacted other than standing on her front stoop gaping as Royce's car drove away from her. She should've screamed at him, told him that he was too practical for his own good. She should have grabbed him by that bow tie and kissed him, reminding him what he was giving up. But of course, she hadn't done any of that. What she had done was carry the stupid *lily-free* bouquet into the house and feed the flowers one by one into her garbage disposal while crying. Like a bouquet was supposed to make up for him shattering her heart?

Did he have any idea how much he'd meant to her? But she knew the answer.

No. He didn't. She'd never told him. She couldn't decide if that made her smart or infinitely stupid. After she'd rid herself of the flowers she curled up with a blanket on the couch and watched TV, desperate for distraction. She cried then, too.

Gia's house looked enormous from the street, but seemed even bigger from the side of the pool where Taylor lounged in a sun chair. It was warm for April—nearly eighty—and the pool was heated. Taylor didn't plan on getting wet, though. It took all her effort to sit here and not seem miserable.

"Spiked lemonade. Perfect for today," Gia announced, swishing outside in a long white cover-up, her bikini revealing each of her enviable curves. "Veggies and hummus?"

"Sure." Taylor forced a smile.

"Okay. Let me traverse through my *enormous* kitchen and see what I can find." Gia had jokingly referred to this house as her "mansion" when she and Jayson bought it. After they divorced, Gia stayed in the house. She'd kept everything, or, more accurately, Cooper hadn't taken anything when he left.

Taylor thought of her own situation and frowned. If she'd been married to Royce and then he'd left her, she'd have sold their shared house in a blink. How could Gia be happy in the house she'd bought with her ex-husband?

Despite the sunny day, clouds hovered over Taylor's mood. Her mind on--who else? Royce.

The jackass.

Tears threatened but she swallowed them down.

They'd been blessed with a bright sunshiny day, sparkling blue water, and she now had a pink cocktail with fruit floating in it. She would force a good mood today if she had to. She sipped her spiked pink lemonade, glad for the token amount of alcohol to numb her feelings. Not that a few ounces of vodka in the slim glass would come close to achieving "numb," but every little bit helped.

Gia returned from the house, a plate of vegetables and hummus in one hand. "You know, I wanted to do this last week, but I was so crampy and bloated and pissy, I decided the only company I should keep was my own." She capped that statement with a smile, and Taylor was surprised to hear herself chuckle in response.

"Don't worry, we only have to deal with Mother Nature's ultimate prank for another twenty or twenty-five years," Taylor said.

In her own lounger, Gia leaned her head back. "Don't remind me. It's not like I'm anywhere near wanting kids now anyway. Why must I have to endure that joyous monthly reminder that I haven't had any yet?"

And isn't that exactly what Taylor had told Royce? She wasn't ready yet. But according to him he wasn't ready *ever*. Maybe she should have talked to him about what he wanted in the future—before he'd come to tell her they didn't have one. Maybe she should've told him she loved him as soon as she knew it herself.

Though, if she'd done that, the breakup would've happened sooner. *And while we were naked.* Hopefully one day she'd look back and understand why they didn't work out, and that him breaking up with her was for the best. But today was not that day.

"Oh! Remind me before you leave to show you the print advertising concepts for the T13. They are *amazing*!" Gia described the ads with a flourish and Taylor tried to listen, but another thought had crawled around to the front of her consciousness.

The thought was a question.

When was her last period?

And because she couldn't recall right away how long ago it'd been, or the last time she'd bought a box of tampons, a frisson of panic laced itself around her ribs.

Royce and Taylor had been careful. Very careful. He'd been the one to remember the protection. She'd usually been hovering around cloud nine after an orgasm, though, which meant something could have been overlooked. Condoms weren't 100 percent effective, either—now, were they?

God.

How long *had* it been? She'd been so busy. So distracted…

Gia sat up from her lounger and removed her sunglasses, tucking them into the messy bun on top of her head. "Are you ready to talk?"

"Am I— About what?"

"You're so sad I can feel it like I can feel this sunshine, sweetheart. I was stalling to see if you wanted to bring it up."

"That's not like you." But now that Gia offered to talk about it, Taylor wasn't going to lie about what had happened.

"You're dating my brother and I love you both, so I'm trying to let you two work it out without my involvement."

"I love him, too." Admitting it out loud made Taylor's heart fracture. Damn Royce and his stupid breakup flowers.

Gia's smile lifted her cheeks. "Really?"

"Yes. But he doesn't love me. He broke up with me yesterday."

"What? Why? Like he can do better?" Ire washed away her friend's smile. What was left was Mama Bear Gia. But then her tone softened and she leaned forward a smidge. "Honey, are you okay?"

Taylor shook her head, tears causing her vision to swim. She wiped her eyes beneath her sunglasses. Gia noticed and was next to her in an instant.

"I am going to kill him. I swear." She stroked Taylor's arm. "I already threatened his person if he hurt you. So he should expect it."

"Maybe we were never a good match from the start," Taylor said around a sob. "We were good together, but I want a future that he says he can't imagine. He can't see past CEO. I deserve better than that."

"Damn right you do."

"I'm incapable of being as pragmatic as Royce. I can't outline our relationship in a flow chart. I can't form an opinion based on past occurrences. I fell in love with him. That had nothing to do with pragmatism."

Gia sighed. "Don't I know it, hon."

"Anyway." Taylor sniffled. "He didn't fall in love with me. That's hard to accept. But even worse was that he wasn't willing to try."

Despite Gia's assurances that Taylor deserved better than someone who had to "try" to love her, Taylor felt like her heart was in pieces at their feet. Or at the bottom of Gia's swimming pool. Today, despite her best efforts, she wasn't going to be able to enjoy the sunshine or her pink drink or her friend's plucky sense of humor. Today she was going to have to sit with her heavy emotions and deal with them the same way she would be dealing with them in the future.

Alone.

Twenty

Taylor waited until the following week to confirm that she was, in fact, pregnant.

Waiting had not ushered in her period. She didn't tell Gia—she didn't tell anyone. She'd gone to the pharmacy, purchased three pregnancy tests and took every one of them. The boxes said to wait two minutes for results, but the pair of "you're pregnant" lines appeared instantly for her.

Rocked as she was, she'd called in sick Monday and had gone to her doctor to confirm. She even had a due date. November 27.

She supposed calling in sick was the truth. She'd been sick at the idea of seeing Royce again. It was almost unbelievable that a month had passed. Since then, he'd been cordial, stiff lipped and mostly absent.

He must've taken every off-site meeting or opportunity to leave the building because his office door had been locked, the room dark most of the time. So many huge changes lay like fallen soldiers between them. Jack had retired. Royce had become CEO. Taylor had found out she was expecting a baby.

She didn't have the luxury of avoidance the way Royce did. In a month or so, her body would reveal the telltale pregnancy bump and everyone would know. Unless she quit her job, there'd be no way to hide it—a moot point since she was keeping the baby.

There were a couple of musts in her life. One, thriving at ThomKnox. Two, keeping her friendships with Brannon and Gia, who were more like family than friends. Taylor wasn't sure where Royce fit in yet, but she'd made a decision about being a mother and it was only fair to give Royce an opportunity to decide how involved he wanted to be in his child's life. Which meant she needed to tell him there was a decision to *be* made.

Sigh. Life was hard.

She'd never been at once so filled with joy and devastation. She missed Royce, but the idea that her family would be starting, granted a lot sooner than she expected, filled her with unmitigated happiness. At the same time, she was sad that her father would never meet his grandchild. And then there was the overall feeling of solitude, since she hadn't told anyone about the pregnancy.

Telling Royce was the number one item on her agenda today.

She approached his office, surprised to encounter a woman sitting outside of it. She was fifty-something at best guess, her hair and clothing stylish. A smattering of freckles dotted her cheeks, giving her an air of youth, unlike the glasses perched on her nose.

"May I help you?" the woman asked with a stiff smile.

"Hi. I'm Taylor Thompson. You must be Royce's new assistant?"

"Executive assistant," she corrected.

"Welcome to ThomKnox." The woman didn't respond, so Taylor kept talking. "So, if he's in, I need to speak with him."

"He requested not to be bothered, but I can let him know you were here." She pulled a pen and notepad from a drawer and looked up at Taylor expectantly.

"This is important, so I'm going to have to insist." Taylor wasn't in the mood to be delayed. She was tired. She was cranky. She was pregnant. She stepped toward Royce's office door, but the woman stood to block her path.

"I'm the COO of this company," Taylor told her.

"I understand, but his instructions were implicit."

"Not to see me?" Taylor hoped not. That was horrifying.

"Not to see anyone, ma'am."

"You're new here," Taylor responded with a patient smile. "You don't understand how things work. Royce will want to hear what I have to say and it can't wait." When she reached for the door handle, the other woman physically swatted her hand away.

"You will not go in there." The woman arched a prim blond eyebrow. "Not while I'm stationed here under orders. No matter who you are."

Red faced, patience lost, Taylor leaned in. "What about if I'm the mother of his unborn child?" she growled. "Can I go in then?"

At that moment, the office door popped open. Royce looked from his new assistant to Taylor, frozen in place.

"Sir?" The woman addressed him.

"At ease, Melinda." His calm facade returned. He was too good at calling up that blank look when he needed it. "Taylor. Come in."

That wasn't how she'd wanted him to find out, but there was no going back now. He shut the door behind her and gestured to the leather sofa in his office. He lowered into the chair across from it rather than sit next to her.

"She's intense." Nervous, Taylor smoothed her hands over her skirt.

"I guess I should have been more specific about who to exclude from that request."

"Would I have been excluded?"

His brow furrowed. "Of course."

She supposed that was some relief. At least he didn't hate her. "I have three positive pregnancy tests and a report from the doctor in my purse." She took the bag off her shoulder and began riffling through the contents.

"Not necessary." He stayed her with a hand. "I believe you."

"I didn't do this on purpose."

"I don't think that," he said calmly. He was too calm for her liking. She didn't know what kind of reaction she expected, but it wasn't this.

"I'm keeping the baby. You'll be involved in your child's life if you want, of course. I'd never shut you out. But I understand you're busy and I know that your new position as CEO is demanding. I'm prepared to do what it takes to continue my own position here, including working from home on occasion after the baby is born."

Royce blinked. "Okay."

"Your level of involvement is totally up to you. I won't saddle you with a family if you're not ready." And according to the last visit he'd paid her on her front stoop, he wasn't anywhere near ready.

He dipped his head to acknowledge her. Silence fell, the only sound Melinda's voice through the door when she answered the phone.

The tide of emotions—anger, sadness, loss—could be blamed at least partially on Taylor's physical state. Hormones caused tumultuous emotions, right? She refused to cry in front of Royce. Even though he'd broken her a little. Hell, maybe a lot. The fallout wasn't complete yet. But she wouldn't whimper in front of him like a lost puppy. She had to be strong. She'd have a family of her own soon—just the two of them if the shell-shocked expression on his face was any indication of how well he was taking the news.

"We have time to sort out the details," she said, hoping to prompt a response.

"Okay," was all he said.

"Okay," she repeated. "Well. I guess I'll be going."

He followed her to the door, his eyes on her purse as she pulled it over her shoulder.

"Hopefully leaving will be easier than coming in," she sort of joked.

"I'll let Melinda know you can come in anytime you like," he said. "Maybe I'll even include Bran and Gia on that list."

Neither of them smiled as he pulled open the door.

"Thanks for coming by," he said formally when she stepped out. Hopefully he'd said that for Melinda's benefit. Him being this distant, this cold, this unresponsive was awful.

She was the woman who'd once drawn a response from him that was borderline out of character. She'd kissed him in a closet two months ago and uncovered a man neither of them had known existed. Not only had they not returned to the way they were before the kiss, but they'd arrived in a place they'd never been. With her as cordial and distant as he was.

Awful. Just awful.

Back in her office, she sat on her chair and stared blankly at the computer screen. Then she logged on and opened her email and started working.

Maybe what they needed was time apart. Time to digest that they'd soon be parents. And judging by Royce's reaction—time to accept that they'd be parenting apart as well.

Twenty-One

Time should have quelled the pain.

It should have, but it hadn't.

Royce had turned over the last personal conversation he'd had with Taylor every day since it'd happened, and had arrived at the same exact conclusion every time.

He'd blown it.

She was pregnant and he hadn't reacted well to that news, either. To learning he was going to be a father and could "choose his level of involvement." Like this was a video game and he had the option to choose his starting level. In his defense, he hadn't had time to react considering he'd had an audience—his tart assistant. Had he been eased into the news rather than overhearing it, maybe his reaction would have been more favorable. Then again, who the hell knew? He had zero experience hearing he was going to be a father before last week.

God. A baby. The fact that he would soon be a parent to a living, breathing human being still hadn't sank in. Probably because he was excellent at compartmentalizing.

The baby wouldn't be born for months. No reason to rush to a decision. Plus, he'd told Melinda not to disturb him because he'd had a packed week ahead of him. It hadn't been hard to fill his time with myriad tasks considering he was still wearing the CFO *and* CEO hats.

Though now that he'd completed his round of interviews with three very qualified candidates for the position of Chief Financial Officer, and the follow-up interviews were scheduled with Brannon and Taylor, Royce was left with a lot of time on his hands. With nothing but quiet in his head so that he could figure out how he felt.

How *did* he feel?

Elated.

Devastated.

Buoyant.

Enraged.

Ridiculously happy.

But that happiness was a balloon that couldn't fully inflate, as if there was a microscopic pinprick letting out a stream of air. Arguably he was the "prick" in this case. Which pissed him off more.

He'd funneled that anger, that rage, and aimed it

directly at the version of Taylor in his mind. How dare she make plans and exclude him? She'd told him he could be involved as if it was optional. Like he would be too busy to spend time with his son or daughter?

Son.

Daughter.

He'd have one or the other come winter. It was terrifying. Exciting.

Inevitable.

Bran let himself in without so much as a knock, interrupting a rare bout of silent time and earning a solid scowl from Royce.

"I waited until Melinda went to lunch to sneak in." Bran shuddered theatrically. "She's scary."

"She's thorough. What do you want?" Royce asked, tired. "If this is about the follow-up interviews, I'll indulge you."

"It's about Taylor."

"In that case, you can go." Royce was only half kidding.

"Much as I'd like to leave you alone with your righteous anger," Bran said as he lounged in a chair in front of Royce's desk. "I'm going to have to call you on your bullshit."

"Did you misunderstand me? I don't want to talk about Taylor with you."

The pregnancy was common knowledge. Not only did Melinda and anyone within earshot overhear Taylor, but Royce had immediately told his siblings. Gia was hurt that Taylor hadn't come to her, but Royce wasn't taking his chances where his brother and sister were concerned. The last time he'd kept a secret from them, it'd blown up in his face.

"Taylor informed me that I can choose my level of involvement. As if my *not* being involved was an option," Royce grumbled anyway, ignoring his own earlier statement that he didn't want to talk about it. The truth was he *did* need someone to talk to. "How could she say that to me? Did what happened between us mean so little to her?"

Bran laughed, which sent Royce's anger soaring. "Do you hear yourself, man? How much could she possibly have meant to you if you dumped her on her doorstep?"

"I did what had to be done."

"Listen, I'm as surprised as you are that Taylor is expecting your baby. But can you blame her for making a plan? Her life is about to change irrevocably."

"Well, so's mine!" Royce roared.

"Gia thinks you're lucky Taylor told you at all."

"Oh, you and Gia are talking about it now, too? Maybe the three of you should get together, decide my part and let me know."

"Don't be pissed at me. I happened to be there while Gia was ranting about what a moron you were. You know I always love a good conversation about what a moron you are." Bran smiled, but then quickly grew serious. "Do you have any idea how miserable you've been lately, or have you been ignoring that too?"

"I'm fine." If *fine* felt like he'd lost the outermost

layer of his skin or like his heart had been mashed into paste with a crowbar, then sure, Royce was fine.

"You were *fine* when you were dating her," Bran said. "Or didn't you take time away from your busy schedule long enough to notice?"

His brother picked the wrong moment to needle him. Typically, Royce was able to be the bigger man. He knew when to let things go, and when to pursue them. He was the ultimate at picking his battles. Just not today.

"You don't get to do this, brother," Royce said, his voice low. "Not while I'm grappling with impending fatherhood. Not while I'm trying to hire a new CFO—a role that was mine for a decade plus. Not when I'm reeling over the woman I love not caring if I'm involved in our child's life or not!"

The door to his office opened and Gia stood in the doorway, wide-eyed, her hand resting gingerly on the handle.

"Hey, sis." Royce leaned back in his chair and threw the pen he'd been holding onto the desk. "Come on in and have a seat. Or should I call a staff meeting and announce to everybody what I'm going through?"

She traded wary glances with Bran, and then they both turned their eyes to their older brother.

Royce, beyond frustrated, huffed one word. "What?"

Gia's eyebrows rose.

"Why are you both staring at me?" Royce tried again.

"The woman you *love*," Gia said. "You heard that,

right?" She elbowed Bran's arm without looking at him, instead studying Royce like he was a specimen in a petri dish.

"I think I heard it. I'm stunned stupid." Bran blinked.

Royce didn't know what the hell either of his younger siblings were talking about. What he didn't need right now was either of their opinions. What he needed was for them to leave him alone so he could—

Love.

Had he said that?

"Oh my God," Gia said to Bran. "I'm pretty sure he just realized what he said. Do you think he didn't know before we pointed it out?"

"I'm not sure. Let's watch and see what happens." Bran folded his arms and stared at his brother. Royce's collar felt hot. His bow tie, usually nestled comfortably in that collar, was strangling him. Cutting off the blood supply operating his brain.

He hadn't been using his brain during that outburst. He'd been speaking from his heart. And his heart had definitely not consulted his brain before those words had exited his mouth.

"I'm in love with Taylor," he said for the first time out loud. Admitting it to himself while admitting it to his brother and sister. "I've been miserable without her. I felt like… Like I was sinking, with cinder blocks tied to my feet. No matter how hard I struggled to pull myself to the surface, the weight kept pulling me down."

"Sounds like love to me," Gia said softly. Her saying anything softly was a rarity, so Royce paid attention. "I felt like that after my divorce. I'd like to tell you it gets better. I want to tell you that the sinking, drowning feeling fades. I don't think it does. I think you just learn to think about it less often. To grab little bits of air when you can."

"Meanwhile, I wish I could tell you that you deserve this. That you entered territory you shouldn't have gone anywhere near." Bran shook his head. "But I can't. Taylor did something to you. She changed you. In a good way. Even though I'm the one who suggested you break up with her."

"You ass!" Gia punched Bran in the arm.

"Ow! I know, okay?" Bran rubbed his arm, grumbling about Gia's pointy knuckles before turning back to Royce. "My point is that a baby…a baby is a big deal. And if you're in love with the woman carrying your baby… Royce. You're going to be a father."

"You're going to be a daddy," Gia sang in a syrupy voice. "I'm going to be an aunt. I was upset Taylor didn't tell me about the pregnancy tests at first—that I had to hear it from you, of all people."

"Hey." Royce frowned.

"I was being selfish," Gia continued. "This isn't about me. Taylor dealt with the news the best way she knew how. You should be glad she isn't cutting you out of your life."

"That's Taylor. Selfless," Bran said, and Gia nodded her agreement.

"Putting herself last," Royce added. "She was trying to make this easy on me. I didn't deserve it."

"That's true," his sister said. "But you can always make it up to her."

"Have you decided what you want?" Bran asked Royce. "Taylor's letting you choose your level of involvement. Did you?"

No.

He had compartmentalized. He'd ignored everything but work. He *hadn't* dealt with it. And he clearly needed to deal with it. He'd had no idea what was in his head or his heart until his outburst.

"I need the room." Royce stood and walked to the door. "Please."

Bran and Gia filed out, Bran slapping Royce on the shoulder as he left. "Sorry."

"Don't be." Royce would figure out something. He wasn't sure what yet, but there was no way he was living his life without the mother of his child. Without the woman he loved. He would figure out a way to win her back—to erase this painful memory and replace it with only good ones.

His cell phone chirped a reminder for the advertising conference call starting in five minutes. The last of the details before the launch. Horrible timing. Every time he turned around, he was putting his life on hold for ThomKnox.

There was a tired argument in the back of his mind about how this was his legacy and how he had to be here, that without him, ThomKnox would go belly-up. Only now it sounded like one excuse on top of another. Royce despised excuses.

Despised that he was making them.

"Fuck it." He tossed his phone onto the desk and shut his office door, locking it behind him.

"Where are you going?" Bran asked as Royce blew by.

"Not here." He stepped into the elevator and pressed the button for the ground floor.

Bran caught the doors before they closed. "What about the conference call?"

"Handle it. I have to do something."

Royce would never forget the look on his brother's face as long as he lived. Pride stretched Brannon's smile as he moved his hand away, his last gesture a nod of confirmation as the doors slid shut.

Royce was through making excuses.

Through living without the woman he loved.

A plan formed as the elevator slid down the shaft and by the time he exited into the lobby of Thom-Knox, his mind was racing along with his heart.

He didn't know if his idea would win her back, but he had to try. His last thought as he climbed into his car was, *I'll try anything. Everything.*

Taylor belonged with him. It was past time he told her so.

Twenty-Two

Taylor loped into her mother's house for dinner, weighed down by everything life had thrown at her over the last month. Not only had Royce been further ignoring her, she'd felt a chill coming from Gia.

Taylor hadn't meant to exclude her friend in the announcement of her pregnancy, but even Gia should understand why Taylor had gone to Royce first.

Gia would come around. Bran had been keeping his opinions to himself and Taylor hoped it wasn't because he'd chosen sides. She wanted her baby to be born into a family overcome with love for their new addition, not upset over how the news was announced.

She'd been battling morning sickness lately too, so when she stepped into the house and the smell of garlic and grilled fish hit her nostrils, her stomach did a barrel roll. She sprinted to the half bath and emptied her lunch into the toilet, gripping the sides of the porcelain bowl.

"Good gracious, Tay!" Her mother rushed in and snagged a decorative hand towel from the ring, wetting it under the sink. Deena helped Taylor to her feet only to push her down on the now-closed lid as she flushed. "What on earth…?"

Deena dabbed the corners of Taylor's mouth, refolded the cloth and patted Tay's overheated cheeks. That mothering gesture was something she'd done when Taylor was young. Deena had always taken care of her. Just like Taylor would take care of her own child soon. With or without Royce Knox.

"What happened? Do you have the flu?" Deena examined her closer and then pressed the back of her hand to Taylor's head. "Not too warm. But you look pale."

Taylor hadn't told her mother yet, and evidently Deena hadn't heard from anyone. Now was as good a time as any. At least Taylor knew her mother would be happy for her.

"I'm having Royce Knox's baby," she announced, looking her mother in the eye. "Fish and I aren't friends right now." Even the word *fish* made her stomach toss. She took the towel from her mother as Deena righted herself. Her mother's face broadcasted five different emotions simultaneously.

Joy won.

"I'm going to be a grandmother? I'm going to be

a grandmother! It's—it's amazing!" She clapped her hands together. "How far along are you?"

"Nine weeks or so. I'm due November 27." Taylor allowed herself to smile, too.

Deena's response was pure and congratulatory. No judgment. Exactly how a mother should react. "Oh! I can make baby announcements! I have the cutest scrapbook paper I've been saving. Yellow ducks! Probably not enough for all the people we'll have to send a notice to, though." She put her hand to her chin in contemplation. "What if we send half ducks and half bears? A few sailboats? Is that tacky? Oh, who cares!" Deena crushed Taylor into a hug and mentioned again how excited she was to be a grandmother.

An hour later, Taylor and her mother finished their dinner—fish free, thanks to her efficient chef. They turned down dessert, and Taylor passed on the port in favor of a club soda with lime.

Only then did Deena broach the subject of—

"And Royce?"

"I'm not sure yet. *He's* probably not sure yet. He's been very…stoic." That was a nice way to say he was acting like a horse's ass. "It didn't work out between us. Before the pregnancy, I mean."

"Oh." Her mother frowned. "You didn't mention it."

"I've been processing."

"I understand. You've been through a lot."

Taylor appreciated her mother not guilting her for keeping her news to herself. That small grace was huge.

"I'm not sure how involved Royce will be. When I told him he kept repeating the word 'okay.'"

Deena clucked her tongue. "Well. You have my support. My undying support."

"ThomKnox is his firstborn. I should have known better than try and compete. I hope he'll make room for one more." She put her hand on her stomach.

"I hope so, too, dear. Your father made room for you. Always."

Taylor's heart grew heavier. "He was a good dad."

"The best," Deena agreed.

They changed topics, Deena discussing the announcements and when to have a baby shower. They ended up in the craft room choosing scrapbook paper with ducks or bears or sailboats, and also a few sheets with little blue whales with starfish stuck to their bellies.

At one point Deena asked if Taylor would like to move back home. The answer was an easy *no way*, but she wouldn't break her mother's heart by saying so. She instead promised Deena ample opportunities to babysit once Taylor returned to work after maternity leave.

Regardless of Gia's reaction, Bran's nonreaction and Royce's *underreaction*, Taylor chose to be happy. And if this pregnancy meant sacrificing the man she loved in order to give her son or daughter an amazing life, then that was exactly what she was going to do.

Twenty-Three

The day of the tablet launch had arrived, and Taylor, while nauseous, made her way into the offices only thirty minutes late.

She hadn't known what to expect on the day of Royce's first product launch, but certainly not what she walked into. Basically the same office she'd left at five o'clock last night. Most of the staff was in their offices, a few chatting casually in the break room. Even Bran waved a casual hello as she passed by.

Royce's office was dark but his aggressive assistant was in her chair, sitting guard outside his door. Taylor had seen his office dark a lot lately, but she didn't expect it today. He should've been here brighter and earlier than any of them. Deciding it wasn't worth the run-in with Melinda, she bypassed his office without speaking.

In her own office, Taylor opened her email and settled in for the day, expecting a meeting alert on her calendar for upper management. There wasn't one, but there was a calendar announcement that alerted her to Royce's absence.

He wasn't coming in at all today?

That was insane. The first product launch of his career as CEO and he bailed? Barring open-heart surgery, she couldn't imagine he'd skip work today. She might question the state of his romantic heart, but she doubted the actual organ was in anything less than working order.

At that moment, someone rapped on her closed office door.

"Come in."

A pretty blonde stepped inside.

"Addi. Hi."

Addison averted her eyes for a moment before meeting Taylor's. "Do you have a moment?"

"Of course." Taylor stood and rounded her desk.

"I won't be long, I just…wanted to apologize." Addison folded her hands primly in front of her periwinkle-blue dress. "I've been awful to you and I'm not quite sure how to make up for it. You might not think I was awful, but it's how I define *awful* for myself. I'm happy for you. For you and your baby. I don't want there to be any ill will between us."

Taylor smiled softly, moved. "I owe you an apology, too. I didn't mean to embarrass you when I pointed out that you and Bran looked good together."

"Oh, don't— That's not—" Addison dismissed Taylor with a quick shake of her head. "Anyway. Thank you for the birthday card and flowers. Belatedly. And congratulations on your pregnancy. Also belatedly. You can count on me if you need anything. I liked it better when we got along."

"Me, too." Taylor liked Addison and was glad there wouldn't be any further discomfort where the two of them were concerned. Plus, points to Addi for addressing the elephant in the room. Taylor hadn't been that brave.

Addi wished her luck on the product launch and left, but before Taylor could shut the door, in walked Gia, with an uncharacteristic look of chagrin decorating her face. Without a word, Gia wrapped Taylor into a hug. It went on for nearly a minute. Taylor hung on to her best friend for purchase and tried to keep the tears at bay. She succeeded, but only because Gia pulled away before emotions overtook her.

"So, I'm a horrible person and I owe you an apology." Gia shrugged matter-of-factly.

"False," Taylor replied. "Your timing is curious. Is there a line forming out there or something?" If so, Royce should be at the front of it—the only person in it, in fact.

"I'm thrilled for you. I was upset that I had to hear about my niece or nephew from Royce instead of my best friend, but that was on me, not you. I shouldn't have been so cool toward you."

Taylor noticed her friend's distance, but Royce was Gia's brother. This entire situation had to have been hard for her, too.

"Royce is your brother. I understand your loyalty to him."

"I'll always choose you." Gia smirked, and even if it wasn't 100 percent true, it was still nice to hear. She chewed on her lip for a second before asking, "Have you spoken to Royce today?"

"No. Why?"

"No reason," Gia answered quickly.

"Do you know why he opted to take off on launch day?" Taylor asked, her suspicion rising.

"I don't." Gia's eyes were shifty, her lips buttoned tight.

"Maybe I'll check with Bran. God knows Melinda won't give me any information."

"Good idea," Gia said, not offering any details. "I have to go. It's not every day we launch a new tablet." She rushed out of the room.

That was strange. And the second time in as many minutes that Taylor had been approached by someone who wanted to make amends.

Taylor followed her out, heading to Bran's office next. "Do you also have an overdue apology for me?"

"Sorry, toots. We covered that already." He winked. He wasn't wrong. There was nothing between them but a solid friendship, one she treasured.

"Why is Royce out? I know you know."

"He's at home." Bran looked her straight in the eye.

"Called me this morning and said he was taking off the rest of the week."

"The rest of the *week*?"

"Yep, left his cell phone here and everything."

"It's his first product launch!" Had Royce gone crazy? This was the most important release of his career, and if not the most important *ever* at least the most important *right now*.

"He's not okay. And if you don't know why, then you never really knew my brother."

Well. She certainly didn't appreciate that.

"Maybe you should go check on him."

She folded her arms over her breasts. "Did he ask you to tell me that?"

"Nope." They had a miniature standoff.

"He's mad at me," she guessed. "Is he not show-ing up because he's mad?"

"Nope." Bran's eyebrows raised.

"Is he sick?" The calendar didn't specify that he'd taken a sick day, but maybe he didn't want anyone to know.

"Sort of," Bran answered, his tone gentle. "Not the way you think, though. He's sick about a lot of things."

"He's not the only one. Morning sickness is my new BFF."

Bran stood and came to her. "I'm sorry things have been strained between you two. I'm not sure Royce knows what to do with so much change this quickly. And before you challenge me on it," he said when she opened her mouth to offer another *me too*. "I know you've had a lot of change, too. You should know that when Royce came over to break up with you, I might have encouraged him to do it."

"What?"

"Unintentionally," he added. "I was concerned you two weren't on the same page. That you were developing feelings for him. I was also pissed off at him for not telling me he was named CEO the second he found out. It was immature."

"And you blacking his eye wasn't?"

Bran smirked. "That was an accident."

"Uh-huh. I'm not allergic to lilies, by the way. I just don't like them."

"Oh."

"Yeah, 'oh.' You don't know everything." But as much as she wanted to lay into Bran for his contribution, she couldn't. "Not that I blame you. The decision Royce made was ultimately his. You can't make that man do anything he doesn't want to do. He chooses what's most important to him."

Bran smiled at that—an out-and-out grin. "You're exactly right. He prioritizes those he loves. You know, I could actually use your help. Can you go to him? Remind him how important it is for him to be here today? I'd hate for him to wreck the role of CEO now that he has it. You have a better chance of convincing him to come in than I do."

"I don't know…" Bran was her friend. This company was important. But what good would it do for her to go to Royce's house if he didn't let her in?

"You're the COO. Second in command," Bran reminded her. "There's no one else."

"Low blow." Bran knew how much this position meant to her. She wasn't willing to shirk on her responsibilities any more than she would let Royce do it. "Fine. I'll do what I can to flush him out of hiding. But you owe me."

"I owe you," Bran agreed, palms up in surrender.

Royce could blow up his personal life but she wouldn't allow him to take ThomKnox with him. This company meant too much to him—to all of them—and she wouldn't be the reason, even inadvertently, that the CEO didn't do his job.

Twenty-Four

In Royce's driveway, Taylor gaped at the sheer amount of boxed furniture sitting in the open garage. A desk, chair and several bookshelves in flat-pack boxes, leaned in a stack on the wall opposite Royce's sports car.

She walked through the garage and into the house, where she found more boxes, packing foam peanuts scattered over the floor and discarded plastic. One box showed a photo of a bassinet, another box contained a playpen, and yet another, a high chair.

She picked her way around the mess, through the living room and past the couch where she and Royce had first made love. And then toward one of the back hallways where she heard what sounded like an electric drill.

Followed by a very loud swearword.

"Royce?" she called, but the drill was whirring again, her voice lost under the sound. She followed the noise to one of the back bedrooms, and found him sitting on the floor, the remnants of what might have been a crib, if he were handier with a drill, lying around him like giant matchsticks. He looked up at her, visibly stunned to see her there.

He wore a gray T-shirt and light blue jeans, his hair in disarray, she guessed from pushing his fingers through it. She didn't think she'd ever seen him like this. The T-shirt and jeans, sure, but never disheveled. Never with dark pockets under his eyes suggesting he'd been up all night worrying, and never with naked, pained vulnerability reflected in his eyes.

"Taylor." There was enough shock in his voice that she knew Bran had told her the truth. Royce hadn't been expecting her.

"It's ThomKnox's first launch day with you as CEO. What are you doing?" she asked.

"I could ask you the same thing." His smile was crooked as he gestured with the drill. "I'm putting together a crib. *Trying* to put together a crib."

By the looks of it, he wasn't doing a very good job.

"I'm a shitty carpenter."

"Why are you putting together baby furniture?"

His eyebrows pulled together. "Because we're having a baby."

We.

The fault line in her heart was quaking, like she might achieve a ten on the Richter scale from whatever he said next. Falling apart wasn't an option. Nothing had changed, not really. Sure, Royce had bought baby furniture, and was having some sort of breakdown given he was assembling it instead of going to work, but that only proved he'd decided to take responsibility for being a father. It was good news, but it didn't change their relationship.

Though none of his behavior should surprise her. She hadn't expected him to deny responsibility for his own child. Maybe he'd just needed time to process.

"Now it's your turn," he said. "What are you doing here?"

She glanced around the room—at the torn box and Styrofoam, the miscellaneous pieces and a well-wrinkled instruction book. What was she supposed to say?

"It's okay. I should probably go first anyway." He straightened from his crouched position and set the drill aside. He was taller than she remembered him. More capable.

It was her heart that reached out first; the love she felt for him still so prevalent. She hadn't been at his side for over a month. One long, miserable month while she'd decided how to handle a pregnancy on her own—without him. How to handle her life without him. It was proving much harder than she'd imagined.

"So, I was wrong. That's the gist of it," he said, sliding his hands into his back pockets. "My priorities were out of order. I thought ThomKnox came first. I thought loyalty to my family came next—my father, my siblings." He shook his head sadly. "You, Taylor, are the one who comes first. I've never… This is embarrassing…" He trailed off for a moment. "I've never been in love before. I've always been the practical one. The responsible one in my family. Love seemed frivolous. An indulgence. I never gave myself breathing room because I didn't want to let everyone down. It was the role I gave myself, I suppose."

She didn't know how she managed a response, but she did. "You were the one with the legacy."

"Yes." He took one step closer to her. "It took me a longer while to realize how wrong I was about that. You, Taylor Thompson, are my legacy. You are the love of my life. I can't celebrate any ThomKnox milestone without you. *We made a baby*. It's a miracle." His smile was bright, like the sun coming out after a long rain. She'd never seen him so happy.

"It is pretty incredible." She felt her lips tip into a smile of their own.

"I should've reacted better when you told me. I just… I had no idea what to do. I was overwhelmed. But now I'm not. Now, I know."

"You know?"

"Yes." He gripped her biceps. "I want to make a life. With you. ThomKnox is important, but I can work from home sometimes if you need me to be with the baby while you're at the office. You don't have to shoulder this alone. I don't want you to be alone. Hell, *I* don't want to be alone. I want you here, with me. In this house. In my life. In my bed."

Oh, how she wanted that, too. Was her dream of a family and Royce loving her too finally coming true?

"That's what the office furniture is for. So you can set up an office wherever you like. If that's at home with our baby, then that's where your new headquarters are. And if you'd rather return to the office, well, then I'll stay home with our son or daughter."

Our son or daughter. That phrase opened her up and laid her bare. How could she say no to the man she loved? He was inside her, still—he'd been a part of her this entire time. Royce was saying not only that he wanted this family, but that he would sacrifice his own legacy to support hers.

"Our paths have always been laid out before us, Taylor. But we don't have to walk the path our fathers intended. We can still honor them, whether they're here or not." He gave her arms a gentle squeeze, tender emotion shining in his eyes. "We can do the job we were put on this planet to do. Mine isn't, as I previously believed, to be CEO. My job is to love you. I'm going to make up for failing at that. I swear."

"You're doing great so far," she whispered. Happiness bloomed in her chest, dangerous and full. He was in love with her? His *job* was to love her? It was everything she wanted to hear, but… "Royce, if you're having some sort of breakdown or early midlife crisis—"

"It's not a breakdown. It's an epiphany. I've always seen the world as black and white. Your father knew that about me—that my inability to handle emotion well was my downfall. That was why he warned you away from me." Royce smiled gently. "What he didn't know was that you, Taylor, had the ability to change me. To open me up to love. You're my first. I also want you to be my last. I'm happier in the gray with you."

Was Royce right? Had her father only been trying to protect her from a future he'd predicted?

"Do you love me, Taylor? That's the only missing piece. That and the sincerest of apologies, which I'll do right now. I'm sorry I broke up with you. I'm sorry I ended what we had without giving us a chance. I said I couldn't envision myself as a family man, but the truth was I never tried. I overlooked the gift you would've given me—your heart. I love you so much. So much I tried to use an electric drill." His throat bobbed in a rough laugh. "We've had separate dreams for too long. It's time we build a new dream together. One that we choose ourselves, not the one predestined for us."

"I like the sound of that." She swiped the tears from her eyes as he pulled her into his embrace. She went, wrapping her arms around him and knowing he was right about them needing to build a dream together. They would change their fathers' plans, but only slightly. They would run ThomKnox their way. Together.

Against her lips, Royce murmured the words she never thought she'd hear from him. "Move in with me. Marry me. Have my baby."

"Okay," she said simply. And it was simple. She loved him and he loved her, and the rest they would make work. But she couldn't let him fail. They had time to work "them" out. His legacy still mattered. "But the launch…"

"Do you think Gia and Bran would let ThomKnox go down in flames?"

"No."

"Do you think if you aren't there, that they'll let you fail as well?" He tipped his head.

"Absolutely not." Bran and Gia were more than friends. They were family. And now that Royce had proposed—soon they would *literally* be family. And soon Royce and Taylor would begin raising their own.

"Neither do I. Besides. I can't go to the office. I have a crib to build."

"And a bassinet." She let out a soft laugh. "Why didn't you hire somebody to do all of this?"

"I wanted you to see I'm capable of being the man you need me to be. I'll be a good father, Taylor. Like mine. Like yours."

"I know you will. I always knew you would. I'm sorry I ever made you believe otherwise. I love you."

"I love you." He kissed her. She'd never doubted his ability to love his child. She'd only doubted herself. The day he'd brought her those doomed flowers, she should have told him she loved him. She wondered if he would've known then that he loved her.

"I'll be a better husband than I was a boyfriend," he told her. "When I put my mind to something, I always succeed. And with your love in my corner, how could I possibly fail?"

She kissed him, tasting the resolve on his tongue, feeling the passion in his touch. Surrendering to him when he carried her into the next room and they made love long and slow. It didn't quite make up for a month apart, but it was a good start.

A good start that would have the happiest of endings.

They'd see to it.

* * * * *

Don't miss Bran's story!
One Wild Kiss
by Jessica Lemmon
Available April 2020!

#2719 SECRET HEIR SEDUCTION
Texas Cattleman's Club: Inheritance • by Reese Ryan
Fashion mogul Darius Taylor-Pratt is shocked to learn he's the secret heir of the wealthy Blackwood family! That's not the only surprise as he reconnects with his ex, diamond heiress Audra Lee Covington. As old passions flare, new revelations threaten everything...

#2720 HEARTBREAKER
Dynasties: Mesa Falls • by Joanne Rock
Gage Striker vows to protect Mesa Falls Ranch from prying paparazzi at any cost—even when the press includes his former lover, Elena Rollins. Past misunderstandings fuel current tempers, but will this fire between them reignite their attraction?

#2721 JET SET CONFESSIONS
by Maureen Child
Fiona Jordan is a professional fixer and her latest job is bringing billionaire Luke Barrett back to his family business. As she goes undercover, the sparks between them are instant and undeniable. But she learns not everything is easy to fix when Luke discovers her true identity...

#2722 RECLAIMING HIS LEGACY
Louisiana Legacies • by Dani Wade
Playboy Blake Boudreaux will do anything to protect his family...including seducing the beautiful philanthropist Madison Armantine to get back a beloved heirloom. But as the secrets—and desire—between them grow, he'll have to reveal the truth or lose her forever...

#2723 ONE NIGHT WITH HIS RIVAL
About That Night... • by Robyn Grady
After a night of passion, smooth-talking cowboy Ajax Rawson and successful life coach Veda Darnel don't expect it to happen again...until it does. But will old family business rivalries threaten to end their star-crossed romance before it even begins?

#2724 THE DATING DARE
Gambling Men • by Barbara Dunlop
Jilted by their former lovers, friends James Gillen and Natasha Remington vow to reinvent themselves and maybe find love again in the process. But their daring new makeovers reveal a white-hot attraction neither was expecting...

*Gage Striker vows to protect Mesa Falls Ranch from
prying paparazzi at any cost—even when the press includes
his former lover, Elena Rollins. Past misunderstandings
fuel current tempers, but will this fire between them
reignite their attraction?*

Read on for a sneak peek of
Heartbreaker
by USA TODAY *bestselling author Joanne Rock*

Elena Rollins stepped toward him, swathed in strapless crimson silk and
velvet. Her dark hair was half pinned up and half trailing down her back,
a few glossy curls spilling over one bare shoulder. Even now, six years
later, she took his breath away as fast as a punch to his chest. For a single
devastating instant, he thought the smile curving her red lips was for him.

Then she opened her arms wide.

"April!" Elena greeted Weston Rivera's date warmly, wrapping her in a
one-armed embrace like they were old friends.

Only then did Gage notice how Elena gripped her phone in her other
hand, holding it out at arm's length to record everything. Was it a live
video? Anger surged through him at the same time he wondered how in the
hell she knew April Stephens.

"Were you unaware of Elena's day job?" Gage asked April as he
plucked the device from Elena's red talons and dropped it in the pocket of
his tuxedo jacket. "She's now a professional menace."

Elena rounded on him, pinning him with her dark eyes. They stood
deadlocked in fuming silence. "That belongs to me," Elena sniped, tipping
her chin at him. "You have no right to take it."

"You have no right to be here, but I see you didn't let that stop you from
finagling your way onto the property."

She glared at him, dark eyes narrowing. "My video is probably still
recording. Maybe you should return my phone before you cause a scene
that will bring you bad press."

Extending a palm, she waited for him to hand it over.

"If you have a problem with me, why don't you tell it to the security team you tricked into admitting you tonight?" He pointed toward the door, where two bodyguards in gray suits were stationed on either side of the entrance. "You're trespassing."

"Is that a dare, Gage?" Her voice hit a husky note, no doubt carefully calibrated to distract a man.

It damn well wasn't going to work on him.

"I'm giving you a choice," he clarified, unwilling to give her the public showdown she so clearly wanted to record and share with her followers. "You can speak with me privately about whatever it is you're doing in my house, or you can let my team escort you off the premises right now. Either way, I can promise you there won't be any cameras involved."

"How positively boring." She gave him a tight smile and a theatrical sigh before folding her arms across her chest. "Maybe using cameras could spice things up a bit."

She gave him a once-over with her dark gaze.

He reminded himself that if she got under his skin, she won. But he couldn't deny a momentary impulse to kiss her senseless for trying to play him.

"What will it be, Elena?" he pressed, keeping his voice even. "Talk or walk?"

"Very well." She gestured with her hands, holding them up in a sign of surrender. "Spirit me away to your lair, Gage, and do with me what you will." She tipped her head to one side, a thoughtful expression stealing across her face. "Oh, wait a minute." She bit her lip and shook her head. "You don't indulge your bad-boy side anymore, do you? Your father saw to that a long time ago, paying off all the questionable influences to leave his precious heir alone."

The seductive, playful note in her voice was gone, a cold chill stealing into her gaze.

He'd known she had an ax to grind with him after the way his father had bribed her to get out of his life.

He hadn't realized how hard she'd come out swinging.

Don't miss what happens next in
Heartbreaker
by Joanne Rock, part of her Dynasties: Mesa Falls series!

Available March 2020 wherever
Harlequin Desire books and ebooks are sold.

Harlequin.com

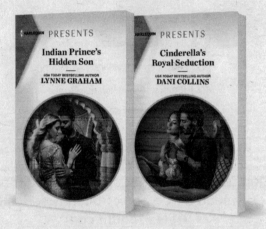

Love Harlequin romance?

DISCOVER.

Be the first to find out about promotions,
news and exclusive content!

Facebook.com/HarlequinBooks

Twitter.com/HarlequinBooks

Instagram.com/HarlequinBooks

Pinterest.com/HarlequinBooks

ReaderService.com

EXPLORE.

Sign up for the Harlequin e-newsletter and
download a free book from any series at
TryHarlequin.com

CONNECT.

Join our Harlequin community to
share your thoughts and connect
with other romance readers!
Facebook.com/groups/HarlequinConnection

HARLEQUIN

HSOCIAL2020